BURNED

Wild Magic Book 2

Danielle Grenier

THE WILD MAGIC SERIES

Book One: Wild Magic

Book Two: Burned

Cover Art by 100Covers (100Covers.com)

Editor: Karen Boston (https://kbostonedit.wixsite.com/kbostonedit)

CHAPTER 1

Alice trudged down the street, frustrated and tired. It seemed like every time she worked the closing shift at the movie theater, some jerk spilled a jumbo-sized soda. She then had to spend the better part of an hour scrubbing the sticky mess and trying to absorb as much of the liquid as possible from the seats. It was supposed to be an easy job to make extra money while she was in college, but it was turning into more trouble than it was worth.

Snap.

Alice jumped at the sound, then paused and looked around, trying to see where it came from. It was dark, but the street she was on was pretty well-lit despite being just on the fringes of what most people considered the "bad" part of town, where abandoned warehouses attracted all sorts of vagrants and criminals. The street was full of older but still pretty decent apartment buildings that were affordable for students. A man down the street was walking his dog, and a car drove by every few minutes, but the street was pretty empty at this time of night. Alice glanced down the alley next to her and squinted, trying to see if anything was down there; nothing looked out of place, so she just shrugged and kept walking. Toronto was well-known for raccoons in dumpsters, and she had no desire to run into one of them.

Alice pulled out her phone as she walked, checking her class schedule for the next day. She'd made it a few more blocks when the hairs on the back of her neck stood up and she stopped suddenly. She looked around but didn't see anything strange. Still, something felt off. Like someone was watching her. She tucked her phone into her pocket and reached into her purse, quickly finding her keychain. She found the little pink cylinder of pepper spray a friend had given her and held it in her right hand, finger on the trigger. Alice picked up her pace, looking left and right as she went, the feeling of being watched staying with her. She told herself it was all in her head, she was just overtired and stressed.

She turned the corner, and as her apartment building came into view, she breathed a sigh of relief – just as something heavy slammed into her from behind, smashing her face against the pavement before she even had time to scream. Pain overwhelmed her as her vision faded to black and she lost consciousness.

CHAPTER 2

The phone rang. Again. Angel didn't even bother to check the Caller ID; she knew who was calling, and she wasn't planning on answering. Not today, and probably not any day in the future. The phone rang a couple more times, then fell silent. She felt a tightness in her chest and set down the rest of her lunch, the sandwich turning dry and tasteless in her mouth. It had been two months since she'd set foot on pack land. Two months since she'd seen Caleb. Two months since she'd been able to work.

After the incident with Jones, she'd been placed on paid leave. The Agency didn't want her using blood magic in the field, as it was way too much of a liability. Angel could understand their caution, but she figured after taking down a former WEA Agent gone black witch, she would have received a little more than a pat on the back and the cold shoulder. So, in an effort to keep herself occupied, Angel prepped her garden for winter, painted her bedroom, studied new spells and potions, and reported once a week for physical and mental evaluations. Her superiors wanted to measure the amount of blood magic she retained, and for how long, and they wanted to make sure she didn't feel the need to go out and get more. Fortunately for her, she had a lot of self-control; her wolf was a hell of a lot stronger than any potential addiction she could find, especially since she was being denied her Mate. For a short while, Angel had imagined she and Caleb might actually have a chance. Unfortunately, a good night's rest and a little distance had made her realize it wouldn't work. Sure, Caleb was attracted to her, but thanks to the ring that hid her scent, he'd never know she was his Mate. She could come clean and tell him she was a hybrid, but once he knew, his family would know. Then his pack. And then it was only a matter of time until she was out to all the wrong kind of people and everyone she ever knew would be at risk. So, they might have a couple weeks, or a couple months, but eventually it would end, and it probably wouldn't be pretty. Her wolf disagreed wholeheartedly, confident the risks were well worth the reward.

Tell him the truth, she urged, *day after day, he is our Mate, he will protect us.*

Angel wanted to believe her other half, she truly did, but she knew it would never work. At first she'd answered Caleb's calls and made excuses for why she couldn't see him, too afraid to deny him outright. Eventually, he'd stopped accepting her excuses, and she'd been forced to lie to him. She told him she didn't want to see him, that they'd had a little fun but it couldn't go any further. Obviously, he hadn't believed her. He continued to call her, at least every other day, and she made the decision not to answer anymore.

She knew eventually Caleb would get the hint and stop trying. Of course, it would be a lot easier if Angel hadn't somehow become best friends with his sister, Sara, almost overnight. The bubbly little wolf called Angel every other day to talk about everything from the weather to sports to how annoyed she was at the males for treating her like a porcelain doll. Given that Sara was eight-and-a-half months pregnant and already looking ready to pop, Angel couldn't really blame them. One thing Angel truly appreciated about her friendship with Sara was the she-wolf never discussed the situation with her older brother.

Angel stared blankly at the spell book she'd been reading, then cursed out loud and tossed a pencil across the room. Her wolf paced inside her head, furious that she continued to ignore their Mate. Knowing she wouldn't be able to concentrate on anything right now, Angel stood up and headed to her bedroom to change into running clothes. With so much free time, and so much anxiety, she'd started running farther and farther every day. Circling her property didn't even wind her, so she took to the rural roads and ran and ran and ran. Some days she completely lost track of time, running until well past dark. The first few times, she'd simply turned around and run home, arriving tired, hungry, and sore. One time, frustrated that she'd lost track of time again, and upset the blood magic in her system wasn't dissipating very quickly at all, Angel had decided to try teleporting home. Surprisingly, it had worked like a charm. One moment she'd been at least thirty kilometers from home, and the next she was in her own back yard. And so, in an attempt to burn off the blood magic in her system, she began teleporting more often, trying spells she wouldn't normally have the power to perform. It was fun for the first few weeks, and eventually some of the spells became difficult for her to manage, but her ability to teleport seemed to stay with her.

Changing quickly, Angel checked the time before heading outside. It was only 1pm, so she still had lots of time before the sun set, even this late in the year. Setting out at a very fast pace, she hoped she could tire out her wolf enough to get a good night's sleep.

CHAPTER 3

Caleb slammed the phone down a lot harder than he'd intended. The sound of cracking plastic made him frown. Lifting the receiver gently, he saw the mouthpiece was crushed beyond repair.

"Damn," he muttered to himself.

"Be nice to the phone, Caleb," Sara scolded from her comfy chair by the fire.

"Yeah, we can't afford to keep replacing them every time you throw a tantrum," Ryan teased.

"Shut it," Caleb growled at his brother. "I'm not in the mood."

"Oh, relax," Ryan said, holding up his hands defensively. "I didn't mean anything by it."

"Don't tease him, Ryan," Sara warned. "Or do you not remember what happened last time?"

The "last time" Ryan had teased Caleb about Angel not answering his calls, the younger wolf had found himself thrown out a second story window. Caleb had apologized, but it didn't mean he wouldn't do it again. Wolves were tough and healed quickly, but it still hurt when they broke bones. Dropping into one of the empty chairs, he sighed deeply. Sara was reading a book, while Wyatt hovered nearby, pretending to read his own book. Ryan was playing some sort of game on his phone that involved hurling birds at pigs.

"Why doesn't she answer?" Caleb asked aloud. He looked to Sara, since she was the only pack member who'd interacted with Angel in the past two months.

Sara sighed, marked her place in her book, and set it down on the coffee table.

"We've been through this already," she said, "I haven't discussed it with Angel. She obviously has her reasons for not wanting to see you, but she's not sharing them with me. The best thing you can do is give her time to figure things out."

"I've given her time," Caleb exclaimed. "I've given her lots of time, and she still ignores me. Did I do something wrong?"

"Women are complicated," Sara explained, "some more than others. You didn't do anything wrong, but you should stop calling her so much, and eventually she'll contact you. Trust me."

"I don't see why you're so hung up on Angel," Ryan commented absently. "I mean, sure she's hot, and she's pretty tough – for a witch – but there's lots of females here who wouldn't dream of ignoring your calls. I mean, it's not like she's your Mate or anything." When Caleb didn't immediately respond, Ryan looked up from his phone and gave him an incredulous look. "She isn't your Mate, is she?"

Sara, Wyatt, and Ryan all sat forward expectantly, while Caleb tried to figure out how to answer. The truth was, he really did have to think about the answer. He'd never been so hung up on a female before; in the past, he and his wolf had been perfectly content to hook up with any of the available females in his pack. As Alpha, it was pretty easy for him to find someone to spend the night with. But since he'd met Angel, he hadn't been with anyone. Her scent had intrigued him from the start, but Caleb had always imagined finding his Mate would be more spectacular - like the world would stop spinning or fireworks would magically appear. With Angel, the attraction was obviously there, but it felt like something was missing. It was strange, and he couldn't explain it, but that was how it seemed to him.

"Honestly, I don't know."

Ryan let out a long whistle.

"Damn. That sucks."

"I'm sure you'll figure it out eventually," Sara told him. "Sometimes these things just take time."

Caleb made a noncommittal sound.

"In the meantime," Ryan said, "I think you need to get out of the house. Get her off your mind for a bit. Tomorrow, we're going out, and we'll find you a nice she-wolf to spend some time with. Or maybe even a human, whatever you want."

"I really don't think that's such a great idea," Sara cautioned.

"It's a great idea!" Ryan assured her. "A night out, and a maybe quick romp to get his head on straight. Get some perspective."

"Caleb, do you really want to go out bar hopping with Ryan?" Sara asked.

Caleb, who'd only been half-listening to his siblings, looked up at Sara's concerned face and Ryan's excited one. "Sure," he replied, then a little more forcefully, "why not?"

"Excellent!" Ryan crowed, standing and slapping his brother on the shoulder. "I'll get the word out – we're gonna paint the town red!"

CHAPTER 4

Angel had just stepped inside the door with an armful of groceries when her phone rang. Fumbling to set down the bags quickly without crushing anything, she managed to pull the phone from her pocket before it went to voicemail.

"Hello?" she answered, belatedly realizing she hadn't checked the Caller ID.

"Angel, sweetheart," her mother's voice rang through the ear piece, "how are you?"

"I'm fine, Mom," Angel replied. "Bored out of my mind, but I'm fine."

"Well, chin up, dear," her mother encouraged her. "I'm sure they'll let you get back to work soon. In the meantime, how would you like to help me out with a little project?"

Elizabeth Myers had this uncanny ability to make something sound like a question when it really wasn't. Angel knew she had two options: either argue with her mother about getting involved with whatever her "project" was and end up helping anyway, or just agree to help now and save herself the trouble.

"Sure," Angel replied dejectedly. "What kind of project?"

"Oh, you'll see," Elizabeth assured her. "Just be at my house tomorrow morning, ten a.m., and be sure to wear something nice."

Again, Angel decided to take the path of least resistance. "Alright, I'll see you then," she said, hitting the "End Call" button and setting the phone down on the counter. As she set about unpacking her groceries, she tried not to think about what her mother would have waiting for her the next morning.

At 10am, Angel pulled into her mother's driveway. She was wearing a dress (because her mother would have made her change into one if she'd worn pants) and holding a very large cup of coffee. Elizabeth greeted her enthusiastically, grabbed Angel's arm, and dragged her through the house and into the back yard, which had been transformed into some sort of Autumn wonderland.

"Uh...wow," Angel said, turning on the spot to get the full effect. Small dining tables dotted the yard, decorated with fake leaves and felt turkeys. A cornucopia sat in the center of each table, spilling fake fruits and vegetables artfully onto the tablecloths. Similar decorations adorned the porch and most of the trees. "What is all this?"

"I'm throwing a little Thanksgiving party," her mother exclaimed, clearly excited.

"But Thanksgiving is next weekend," Angel corrected her.

"I know that," Elizabeth replied, "but next weekend everyone will be spending time with their families, so I figured I would throw my party the weekend before."

"OK, then, where's all the food?" Angel asked, knowing her mother wasn't exactly skilled when it came to cooking.

"Oh, the caterer should be here any minute," Elizabeth replied, fussing with the place settings on the nearest table. "They'll get everything set up, and all we have to do is entertain the guests.

"And the guests would be...?" Angel prompted, mentally preparing herself.

"Just a few friends," Elizabeth replied vaguely.

"Alright, then," Angel said, barely containing a sigh and resigning herself to the fact that she'd probably get introduced to every eligible male before the food was even served. "Anything you need me to help with?"

"Oh, yes, could you please set up some warm spots around the yard? I want to make sure no one gets cold while we're eating."

"Sure thing."

Starting by the back door, Angel set up small spells around the yard that would work like little radiators and ward off the fall chill. It wasn't a difficult spell, but the yard was a decent size, so it took about half an hour to finish. By the time she made it back inside, the caterers were there, working on the final preparations for lunch. It looked like her mother had arranged for a full Thanksgiving meal, and though she didn't agree with extravagance, she had to admit, it smelled heavenly. Unfortunately, any attempts to pilfer a snack were thwarted by her mother, who showed up just as Angel reached for a slice of turkey.

"Wait until lunch," Elizabeth scolded. "Besides, I need you in the back yard to greet guests and show them where they're sitting." She handed her daughter a seating chart. "Use this, but try to look it over now so you don't need to keep checking it for everyone who arrives."

Angel frowned but took the seating chart and planted herself in one of the chairs on the porch. Glancing at the chart, she recognized most of the names as belonging to relatives of Council members. The Warners, one of the most important witching families on the Council, were conspicuously absent. It probably had something to do with the fact that Angel had shot their eldest son two months ago. It had only been a stunning spell, but apparently some people held grudges about that kind of thing. Not surprisingly, Elizabeth had seated Angel at a table with only men. Though she couldn't tell by their names alone, Angel was willing to bet they were all single, and just around her age. It seemed despite her last attempt failing in such spectacular fashion, Elizabeth was still dead set on getting Angel hitched as soon as possible. Resisting the urge to roll her eyes and attempt an escape before any guests arrived, Angel continued to study the seating chart.

An hour-and-a-half and way too many introductions later, Angel was seated at what she mentally called the "singles table." As expected, all her dining companions were young, male, unattached – and if she was being honest, reasonably attractive. Too bad they had absolutely no chance of endearing themselves to her, since her wolf wouldn't even consider the possibility of being with another male now that they'd met their Mate. Regardless of her current internal struggle, Angel decided to play nice, if only to make her mother happy and avoid a fight later on. For the most part, conversation at the singles table had consisted of random pleasantries in-between bites of food.

"Would you like some more lemonade?" Humphrey Abrams asked her, holding up a pitcher of the pink liquid.

"Yes, please," Angel replied, holding out her glass and silently pitying the young man for having such an awfully old-fashioned name.

"Your dress is lovely," Adam Cross commented.

"Thank you," Angel replied, trying to sound sincere. And so it continued throughout the entire meal, or at least until dessert came.

Angel was still hungry, but since her mother had encouraged her not to "stuff her face," she picked daintily at her dessert, promising her half-empty stomach a giant cheeseburger on the way home. She was halfway through the tiny slice of cheesecake when Dean Foster spoke up.

"So," he began casually, "I don't imagine the Warners were invited to this particular event?"

Adam, Humphrey, and Elliot snickered.

"Uh, no," Angel answered cautiously, her stomach sinking at what was going to come next, "they weren't."

"No big loss there," Elliot remarked, and surprisingly, the others nodded in agreement. "If I have to listen to that prick talk about how close he is to getting a Council position, I might be sick."

"Yeah, or maybe we could hear all about his wedding preparations with Jill what's-her-name," Adam added.

"Uh, yeah," Angel said noncommittally, taking a big swig

of her coffee.

"Is it true you shot him with a stunning spell, Angel?" Humphrey asked.

"No, no, no," Dean interrupted before she could answer, "she clocked him - knocked him out cold."

"Where'd you hear that?" Adam asked.

"A very reliable source," Dean replied.

"More reliable than the witch who did it?" Humphrey demanded, gesturing to Angel.

"Uh, look," Angel interrupted before anyone else could speak again, "it was a stunning spell, and it was a rather...uh... delicate situation."

"I knew it!" Humphrey crowed.

"Yeah, yeah, whatever," Dean grumbled, clearly upset that he'd been proven wrong.

"So, Angel," Adam said, turning to her and reaching for her hand. She pulled away before he could do more than brush his fingertips across her knuckles. "Would you like to come to the Autumn Ball with me? I just know Warner's gonna be there, and I bet seeing you would make him scream like a little girl!"

"I don't think so," Angel replied, a little uncomfortable with the direction the conversation was taking.

"Then come with me instead," Humphrey offered. "I know there's a lot of people who would just love to meet you."

"Because I shot William Warner with a stunning spell?" Angel asked, a little incredulous.

"Of course!" Humphrey exclaimed. "You're like an urban legend!"

"Uh, right," Angel mumbled, suddenly very uncomfortable. "Thanks for the offer, but I'm going to have to decline. I, uh, I have to use the ladies room. Please excuse me."

Before any of them could react, Angel was up, out of her seat, and across the lawn. She smiled politely at anyone she passed, but didn't slow down until she made it to the bathroom and locked the door behind her. Leaning back against the door, Angel sighed heavily.

"What the hell..." she muttered to herself. "It's like I'm some kind of attraction."

Before Angel even had the chance to contemplate what her newfound fame would mean, her mother knocked on the door.

"Angel?" she called. "Angel, is everything alright?"

Angel almost replied with a "Yes," mostly out of reflex, before actually considering her answer. Here she was, two months off the job, pining after a man she could never actually be with, and she might as well be the damn centerpiece on the table. Flinging open the bathroom door, she faced her mother

"No," she snapped, "everything is not alright. I'm sick and tired of your silly attempts to find me the 'right' man, when all I am to these people is some cheap novelty. I'm done. I'm going home. Right now."

"Don't be ridiculous, Angel," Elizabeth chastised her. "That's not how they see you at all. Now, why don't you take a minute to calm down, then come back to the party?"

"Not happening," Angel insisted, pushing past her mother and down the hallway. Her mother called after her, but Angel just tuned her out and kept walking.

Later that night, after a couple massive cheeseburgers and more fries than she could count, Angel sat on her couch, watching television. The news was on, the pretty blonde newscaster blabbing on about one thing or another. Her mind kept wandering, trying to figure out the mess that had become her life. At this point, the only thing she could think of that would improve things would be if she could get back to work. Then, she could at least have something to focus on, something to distract her from everything else. Unfortunately, it didn't look like she'd be getting back to work any time soon.

A face flashed across the TV screen she recognized immediately: William Warner. Despite herself, Angel turned up the volume.

"Big news for the magical world in Waterloo today," the

newscaster began, "William Warner has been appointed First Witch for the Waterloo Coven. Mr. Warner will be taking his place as the Coven leader in the upcoming solstice. In other news, another strange attack has been reported in downtown Toronto, with the victim suffering from extreme blood loss. This is the third reported attack in as many months, and -"

Angel abruptly flipped the channel. Her mother was certain to bring up the news about William as soon as possible and launch into yet another tirade about how badly Angel had messed up that relationship. It wasn't like she could help it that William was a pompous idiot with absolutely zero survival skills. If anything, the Warners should have thanked her for saving their precious son. Flipping through the channels, she tried to find something that would distract her long enough to forget her mess of a life. After a few clicks of the remote, she found a suitable program, some sort of reality show where a contestant was working his way through a bucket of worms to try and win money. It turned her stomach a little, but it was a welcome change, at least for now.

CHAPTER 5

Caleb wasn't sure if it was his brother's enthusiasm or the amount of alcohol he'd consumed, but by the second bar of the evening, he was feeling pretty good. A large number of single wolves - both male and female - had come along and were taking up the majority of the tables in the small, dimly lit bar. A live band was playing near the back, and mediocre covers of popular country songs drifted through the air.

"Didn't I tell you this would be fun?" Ryan asked as he returned to the table with a couple beers.

"You did," Caleb admitted.

"And?" Ryan prompted.

"I'm having fun," Caleb allowed, grabbing a beer and taking a long swallow.

"Of course you are!" Ryan beamed proudly.

"Yeah, yeah," Ethan grumbled from Caleb's right, "we get it, you were right, just like you were right at the last place. Now quit your bragging and drink your beer."

Caleb laughed as the smile slid from his brother's face, to be replaced by what could only be described as a sad pout. Glancing around the bar, Caleb saw a number of female pack members he'd slept with in the past. Several of them looked his way and smiled seductively, but only one actually approached him. Sadie was a lovely, tall, blonde wolf with amazing legs. Tonight, she was wearing a tiny skirt that barely covered her ass and a tank top at least two sizes too small for her. They'd had fun together in the past; Sadie was always up for a romp, and she was definitely attractive.

"Alpha," she greeted him formally but ran her red-painted fingernails up his bare forearm at the same time.

"Hello, Sadie," he replied. "How are you tonight?"

"Oh, I'm just fine," she purred, leaning forward slightly to give him a better view of her cleavage. "But I could use a little company. You wanna dance?"

Caleb hesitated, but Ryan took that moment to interfere. "Of course he would," he insisted, pushing his older brother towards the she-wolf.

Sadie wrapped her arm around his and led him towards the dance floor, while Caleb flipped off Ryan behind her back. Sadie pulled him to the center of the open space occupied by other dancing couples, enticingly swaying her hips. Caleb let her take the lead, moving his body in time with the music, but something still felt wrong. He couldn't help imagining what it would be like to dance with Angel.

"What's the matter?" Sadie asked a few minutes later, sensing his distraction.

"Uh, nothing," Caleb answered quickly, "just thinking."

"About what?" Sadie asked, suggestively trailing a fingernail down his chest.

"Nothing in particular," Caleb said.

"Well, maybe I can change that," Sadie replied, taking his hand and leading him to the back hallway of the bar.

It was dark and relatively deserted, and Sadie backed up against the wall, pulling him against her. Her lips went to his neck, licking and nibbling her way up to his ear. Caleb rested his hand on her hips, trying to focus on Sadie, but images of a tough little witch with green eyes danced through his head. When Sadie's lips found his, Caleb's wolf angrily shouted at him.

No! the beast insisted, causing Caleb to break the kiss and step away from her. Sadie looked up at him, confusion in her eyes.

"I'm sorry," he told her, "I have to go." Before she could protest, Caleb moved out of the hallway and headed towards the table where Ryan and the others still sat.

"Back so soon?" Ryan quipped as Caleb grabbed a beer and took a long swallow.

"Shut up," Caleb warned.

"Oooh," Ryan continued, "Sadie looks pissed. What happened, stage fright?"

"I said shut up!" Caleb growled at his brother, and the other males at the table slowly backed away, not wanting to get between the two of them. Ryan raised his hands defensively.

"Sorry!" Ryan apologized. "I didn't mean anything by it. It was just a joke."

"Just drop it, okay?" Caleb said, taking a deep breath to calm himself.

"You got it," Ryan said. The two sat in silence for a moment before Ryan spoke again. "You alright, Caleb?"

"Yes. No. I don't know," Caleb replied, sighing deeply and finishing his beer.

"You want to talk about it?"

Caleb paused before answering. How could he explain his feelings for Angel to his brother when he didn't even understand them himself? The little witch had wriggled her way into his head, then disappeared, leaving him lost and confused. It was beyond frustrating, especially when his own wolf couldn't help clear things up. His animal side wanted Angel, that much was clear, but was it just curiosity, or was it something else? Thankfully, he was saved from having to answer Ryan's question when his phone rang; the Caller ID flashed "Wyatt" on the screen.

Caleb hit the "Answer" button. "What's up?" he asked.

"It's Sarah," Wyatt replied, "she's gone into labor."

"We'll be there in ten minutes," Caleb assured him, hanging up the phone and turning to Ryan. Thanks to their enhanced hearing, his brother had heard everything and was already throwing down a couple bills to cover their tab.

"About damn time," Ryan said, grinning widely.

CHAPTER 6

The phone woke Angel with a start, rousing her from incoherent dreams about wolves and turkeys. It took her a minute to process what was going on, then she grabbed at the handset.

"Hello?" she mumbled into the mouthpiece.

"Angel?" Caleb's voice came through the line, jolting her from half-asleep to wide-awake instantly.

"Uh, yeah," she croaked out, cursing herself for not checking the Caller ID.

"It's Sarah," Caleb told her, "she's gone into labor."

"I'm on my way," Angel replied, jumping out of bed and searching for a pair of reasonably clean pants. "Gimme twenty minutes."

"Okay," Caleb replied, and when it seemed like he was about to say more, she hung up the phone.

After finding some clean clothes and throwing them on, Angel grabbed her purse, fishing out her car keys as she tore through the house and out the front door. Twenty minutes later, Angel pulled up to the main house of the pack compound, grateful very little traffic was on the roads at 3am. Ethan met her at the front door.

"Just in time for all the fun," Ethan told her, gesturing up the stairs. Angel strode quickly down the familiar hallway, pausing a moment before knocking on the last door on the right. Ryan answered the door a moment later.

"Angel," Ryan greeted.

"How is she?" Angel asked.

"Doing well so far," Ryan said. "Come on in."

The outer room was empty, but sandwiches, snacks, and coffee were set out on the kitchen table. The doors to the bedroom were open, and Angel could hear soft voices coming from inside. Caleb's voice was easily distinguished from the others, and for a moment Angel was frozen in place; part of her was terrified to see him after ignoring him for so long, and part of her was thrilled to see him again. Shaking herself slightly, Angel squared her shoulders, blocked out her wolf as much as possible, and strode into the room. Sara was on the bed, propped up with a large stack of pillows, eyes closed while focusing on her breathing. Wyatt sat on the bed to her right, holding her hand tightly and whispering encouraging words. Caleb sat in a chair to her left, looking a little out of place at the moment. He looked up as she entered the room, and hope flashed across his face, quickly replaced by an overly polite smile.

"Angel," he greeted. "How are you?"

"I'm good," Angel lied, giving an equally polite smile.

"You're both awful liars," Sara said, opening her eyes and pinning first Caleb, then Angel with an exasperated look. Unfortunately, it was ruined when she winced in pain.

"Has the doctor seen her yet?" Angel asked.

"Yes," Wyatt answered. "He said she's still a few hours away from giving birth. He said to try and keep her relaxed and he'll be back in an hour or so to check in."

"Ow," Sara complained, "this hurts."

"Angel, do you think you could help?" Wyatt asked hopefully.

"Of course," Angel replied. Skirting around Caleb's chair, she sat on the bed to Sara's left, scooting close to the she-wolf. She then wrapped one arm around her shoulders and rested the other hand on Sara's large belly. "Sara," she spoke softly, waiting for the wolf to open her eyes, "are you ready?"

Sara nodded gently.

"Go for it," she said.

For several months now, Sara had been encouraging Angel to practice using her magic on wolves. Most of the time, Wyatt had ended up the test subject, since he didn't want anyone practicing on Sara, and Angel had completely agreed with him on that point. Luckily, it turned out Angel had no problem working magic on wolves anymore. Whether that was because of the blood magic she'd acquired from Caleb and Ryan or her own genetics helping out, Angel couldn't be sure. Either way, it meant Angel would be able to use her magic to help Sara through the delivery process. Since most drugs didn't work on them, natural birth was pretty much the only option female wolves had, but with a few simple spells, Angel would be able to keep Sara relaxed and reduce her pain. Focusing her magic, Angel released a small wave of magic into Sara that basically acted like a mild sedative and painkiller. Within minutes, Sara was breathing deeply and lying back on the pillows, much more relaxed than she'd been before.

"Thank you," Wyatt said.

"No problem," Angel replied, smiling at him.

Over the past few months, she'd grown to like Wyatt a lot. He was fiercely protective of his Mate, loyal to a fault, and surprisingly, he had a great sense of humor. While Sara had decided early on Angel was going to be her friend, it had taken a little longer to get there with Wyatt, but it was certainly a friendship worth waiting for.

"Now what?" Ryan asked, strolling into the room with a ham sandwich in one hand and a very large cookie in the other.

"Now we wait," Caleb told him.

The doctor, a middle-aged male wolf with graying red hair named O'Hare, returned about an hour later, pleased with how Sara's labor was progressing. He encouraged her to get up and try walking around, suggesting it might help move things along. Together, Wyatt and Ryan maneuvered her to her feet, and Sara began making slow laps around the room. Angel stayed close by, ready to provide magical assistance whenever she was needed.

Caleb was having a difficult time with the little witch so close. Sitting in the chair next to the bed had been too close, so he'd moved to lean against the wall by the door. His wolf urged him to go to her, touch her, hold her, but he wasn't sure how she'd react, and he wasn't about to do anything that might upset his sister. So, he stayed put.

"Hold up for a minute," Sara said, pausing at the foot of the bed, one hand pressed tightly across her middle. Angel slid forward on the bed to rest her hand on Sara's shoulder.

"You okay?" Angel asked, concerned.

"Yeah," Sara replied, "just a really big contraction."

"Do you want to lie down again?" Wyatt asked, hovering next to his Mate.

"No," Sara answered quickly, "the walking is helping, I just need a minute."

True to her word, after a few minutes of breathing deeply, Sara nodded to Wyatt and, with a little help, got moving again. Angel watched her closely as she moved around the room, catching Caleb's eye as Sara moved past him. Angel held his gaze for a moment before quickly ducking her head. While disappointed in her reaction, Caleb couldn't help noticing the blush that spread across her cheeks. Maybe there was some hope yet.

Sitting in that bedroom with Caleb so close was practically torture. Angel tried her best to focus on Sara, but since they were stuck waiting, it was difficult. His scent teased her nose, bringing her wolf to life, not to mention her libido. She had to assume some, if not all, of the wolves in the room had noticed her reaction, but thankfully they were polite enough not to say anything. Angel needed to get some fresh air, but she didn't trust herself to walk past him without doing something crazy right now. Taking a few calming breaths, she turned her attention back to Sara, working through some meditation techniques in her head. After a few minutes, Angel felt a lot more in control and decided to make her move. Climbing off the bed and stretching quickly, she turned to Sara.

"I'm just going to grab some fresh air," she said, "I won't be far."

"Okay," Sara replied, smiling widely despite the late hour.

Angel strode from the bedroom at what she hoped was a normal pace. After browsing the food available, she decided solid food might not be the best idea for the time being and poured herself a large cup of coffee instead. Moving across the room, she quietly opened the door to the patio and slipped outside.

It was still very dark out, and the sun wouldn't be rising for another couple hours yet. It was chilly, and Angel contemplated going back for her jacket, ultimately deciding she didn't want to bother. Weaving a quick spell, she created a warm spot that encompassed most of the patio. Angel leaned on the railing, looking out at the wilderness surrounding the compound and sipping her coffee slowly. Taking a few deep breaths, she felt her wolf calm a little. Angel heard footsteps, then the patio door opened slowly, revealing Caleb. She groaned inwardly, while her wolf perked up instantly.

"There you are," Caleb said, pasting that same fake smile on his face as he stepped onto the patio and closed the door behind him.

"Just getting some fresh air," Angel replied, turning around to avoid facing him. They stood in silence for a minute or so, and Angel could almost hear the thoughts running through his head. She held herself completely still, knowing if he touched her, it would likely be her undoing. Eventually, Caleb exhaled forcefully, then came to lean against the railing as well, choosing a spot about two feet away from her.

"Did I do something wrong?" Caleb asked, not looking at her.

"No," Angel replied, "you didn't."

"Then why don't you want to see me?"

"It's complicated."

"Is it because I'm a wolf?" Caleb asked begrudgingly.

"No!" Angel insisted, setting down her coffee and turning

to face him so he could see the sincerity on her face. "Not at all."

"Then what is it?" Caleb demanded, facing her now.

The look on his face threw Angel and made her pause. His scent told her even more; he was confused and hurt. It killed her knowing she'd done this to him; she'd hurt her Mate. For a moment, she wavered. For a moment, she considered just telling him the truth and dealing with the consequences, whatever they were. But fear raised its ugly head, and she clamped her mouth shut, turning away from Caleb.

"I just can't be involved with anyone right now," she lied, knowing it sounded lame.

"That's the best you've got?" Caleb asked, getting angry now.

"What the hell is that supposed to mean?" Angel barked, getting defensive.

"It's a piss-poor excuse, and you know it," Caleb insisted.

"So what if it is?" Angel hissed at him. "I don't have to explain myself to you. Maybe you just can't handle the fact that there might be a female on this planet that isn't going to throw herself at you!"

"Maybe you're just afraid you can't handle me," Caleb taunted, moving closer.

Angel took a step back, trying to keep her distance from the seething wolf.

"Ha!" Angel shouted, trying to sound confident as he closed the distance between them. "You wish!"

She jumped when her back hit the railing. Caleb planted his hands on either side of her hips, caging her in his arms. He moved forward, his body pressing against hers in a way that sent shivers up her spine. Angel knew she had to stop this before it was too late, but with him so close, she was having trouble remembering why.

"Stop," she said, her voice barely a whisper.

Caleb brought his fingertips beneath her chin and made her look at him.

"Say it like you mean it, and I will," he challenged.

Angel opened her mouth to answer, but no sound would come. Caleb smiled, and her resistance evaporated in an instant. Wrapping her arms around his neck, she pulled him down for a desperate kiss. Their lips met, and the world seemed to stop spinning. Angel felt his hands on her hips, then she was lifted up and set on the railing. She wrapped her legs around his waist and pulled him closer as his hand slipped under her shirt and reached upwards. Just before he reached his goal, the patio door flew open. Ryan opened his mouth to speak but froze when he saw them.

"Uh," he began, but Caleb growled loudly, and he clamped his mouth shut, lowering his eyes.

"Go away!" Caleb rumbled, barely turning away from Angel.

"Normally, I would," Ryan replied, "but, uh -"

He was cut off when Caleb growled again, this time turning on his younger brother. Angel thought she might have to intervene, but then she heard Sara cry out from inside the house. Caleb's head turned sharply towards the sound.

"Sara!" Angel gasped. She pushed him away, jumped down from the railing, and darted inside.

CHAPTER 7

Caleb stood on the patio for a few moments after Angel had gone, temporarily stunned. He'd gone out there to confront her, to find out why she was ignoring his calls. As expected, she'd thrown him some generic excuse that wasn't anywhere near the truth. Beyond frustrated, he'd called her on her bullshit, fully expecting her to break and tell him the real reason. Never in a million years had he expected a shouting match, followed by the best damn kiss he'd ever had in his life. If Ryan hadn't interrupted them, Caleb had no doubt they would have screwed each other right there on that patio.

"Fuck!" Caleb shouted, finally realizing Ryan was still there. His younger brother smiled and held up his hands apologetically.

"Sorry," he said. "I didn't think...I mean, I -"

"It's alright," Caleb told him, taking a deep breath to calm himself. "Let's go." They headed inside, shutting the patio door behind them. "How's Sara?" Caleb asked.

"The doctor says she's close," Ryan replied.

He opened his mouth to say something else, but Sara's scream had them dashing into the bedroom. Sara was splayed out on the bed, Wyatt glued to her right side, Angel glued to her left. Doctor O'Hare was kneeling at the foot of the bed, examining Sara.

"Just breathe, Sara," O'Hare coached, "just breathe. It's almost time to push."

"Fuck, this hurts," Sara shouted.

"Is it safe for me to help her with the pain?" Angel asked the doctor.

"Go ahead," he said, "but don't numb her completely."

Angel nodded, rested her hand against Sara's stomach, and Caleb felt a tingling sensation as the witch used magic to lessen his sister's pain. Sara took a deep breath, relaxing a bit, then turned towards Angel, taking another deep breath.

"Well," the she-wolf said, grinning widely, "I'm sure glad someone's having fun tonight."

She pinned first Angel, then Caleb with a knowing stare. Angel blushed furiously, and Caleb shrugged his shoulders, giving his sister a wink when no one else was looking.

"Alright," O'Hare said from between Sara's legs, oblivious to everything else in the room, "looks like we're ready to start pushing."

"Thank God!" Sara exclaimed, bringing giggles from Ryan and Caleb both. "You think it's so funny," Sara shouted at them, "why don't you give it a try?"

Caleb held up his hands apologetically, not wanting to upset her at the moment. Ryan did the same, mumbling a quick "Sorry" before escaping from the room. Caleb decided to stay, choosing a chair that would keep him out of the way, but close enough to lend his support.

"Okay, Sara," the doctor said, "get ready to push...and now!"

With a deep breath and great yell, Sara pushed through the next contraction. And the next. And the next. Wyatt held her hand despite the crushing, white-knuckled grip she maintained on his fingers. Angel kept her arm around Sara's shoulders, coaching her through the contractions and using a cool, damp cloth to wipe her forehead. After a few more contractions, O'Hare held up his hand.

"Stop pushing for now, Sara," he instructed tersely.

Sensing the doctor's unease, Caleb stepped forward.

"Is everything alright?" Wyatt asked, concern coloring his voice.

"Just a minute," O'Hare said, moving up the bed and using his fingers to press against Sara's belly.

Sara kept breathing deeply, but Caleb could see she

was worried. O'Hare continued poking and prodding her, saying nothing. Pulling out a stethoscope, he pressed the device against her belly, over and over again.

"Is the baby alright?" Sara asked, sounding a little panicked.

O'Hare didn't answer, setting down the stethoscope and moving back between her legs.

"What is it?" Caleb demanded, finally getting the doctor's attention.

O'Hare took a deep breath.

"We should at least be able to see the head by now," he explained calmly, "and now the baby's pulse is weak. I think the umbilical cord might be wrapped around its neck." He turned to Sara, putting on a brave face. "It's probably nothing," he reassured her, "but I want to make sure before we continue."

Sara nodded, scared for her baby's life. O'Hare moved to continue his examination, but Angel stopped him.

"Wait," she said, "I can check. It won't hurt anything, and it'll be quicker."

"Are you sure?" O'Hare asked her.

"Yes," Angel replied, turning to Sara, who nodded her permission.

"Do it," Sara said.

Angel splayed her hand over Sara's belly, took a deep breath, and closed her eyes. The tingle of magic reached Caleb a moment later and stayed as Angel moved her hand over Sara's belly for a minute that seemed like hours. When she opened her eyes, Caleb could see she was worried.

"The doctor's right," Angel said, "the cord is wrapped around the baby's neck, and it's starting to cut off its airway."

"Alright," O'Hare said, "I should be able to get the baby untangled."

"I don't think you should try," Angel said.

"Why not?" Wyatt asked softly, but Caleb could see he was afraid.

"The baby is in an awkward position," Angel explained.

"If you try to move her, you could cut off her airway completely."

Everyone was silent as they digested the information.

"Wait a minute," Ryan said, having entered the room while Angel was talking. "You said 'her.'"

"Oh, shit!" Angel exclaimed, turning to Sara and Wyatt. "I'm sorry, I know you wanted it to be a surprise, but I really couldn't check on the baby without finding out the gender. Oh, I'm so sorry."

Wyatt had a dazed look on his face, while Sara was hovering between smiling and bursting into tears. Before anyone could say anything else, O'Hare piped up.

"If I can't get the baby untangled," he asked Angel, "how do you propose we get her out safely?"

"I can cut the umbilical cord right now," Angel suggested, "using my magic. Then Sara gives a couple good pushes and everything should be fine."

"Are you sure you can do that?" Wyatt asked cautiously.

"Absolutely," Angel insisted.

O'Hare looked to Sara.

"It's your choice, Sara," he told her. "What do you want to do?"

"Angel can do it," Sara replied, without any hesitation.

O'Hare nodded to Angel, who placed her hand over Sara's belly again.

"When I say so," Angel began, "start pushing."

Angel pressed her hand against Sara's belly, trying desperately not to give away how nervous she was. She had no idea how she'd gained Sara's unfailing trust, but she was sure as hell going to prove she deserved it. Taking a deep breath, Angel reached out her magic, located the umbilical cord wrapped around the tiny girl's neck, and with a quick flare of power she severed the cord.

"Now," Angel told Sara, and the she-wolf started to push.

O'Hare waited between her legs, and after the first contraction, he called out happily. "I can see the head! Keep going, Sara." One more contraction, and O'Hare reached up to catch the baby. "The head is out," he said, "one more big push should do it."

Beside her, Sara took a deep breath, and with a great, big shout she pushed hard one last time. O'Hare caught the baby, snatching up a small instrument to clear her airway, and a moment later the newest member of the pack started to cry. Doctor O'Hare wrapped the tiny little baby in a blanket before handing her to Sara. Angel climbed off the bed and stepped back to give them some room. Sara cradled her daughter in her arms, turning so Wyatt could see her as well.

"She's perfect," Wyatt nearly whispered, "absolutely perfect."

"What are you going to call her?" Ryan asked.

"We're not quite sure yet," Sara said, "we never could agree on names, so we decided to choose after she was born."

"She's adorable," Caleb told his sister, moving forward to kiss his sister on the cheek. Reaching down, he took the baby's hand gently between his thumb and forefinger. "Hello there, little one," he cooed.

Sara shifted so she could hand the baby to Wyatt, who held the little girl like she was the most precious thing in the world.

"What about Maya?" Wyatt asked, turning to Sara, who wrinkled her nose.

"I don't think she's a Maya," Sara replied.

"What about Eve?" Ryan suggested.

"I like it," Sara said, "but I don't think she's an Eve."

"Melissa?" Caleb suggested, and Sara made a face.

"Not a chance," Sara told her brother. At Angel's confused look, Sara laughed. "Melissa was a girl I went to high school with. I hated her. She stole my boyfriend in tenth grade."

"Okay, then," Angel said, laughing at the emotion in Sara's voice when she talked about her high school nemesis. "Cassie?"

Angel suggested, the name suddenly popping into her head.

Sara paused for a moment, thinking about the name. She turned to Wyatt, who smiled at his Mate.

"I like it," he said, looking down at his daughter, "it suits her. Cassie." The little girl let out a happy gurgle. "I think she likes it, too!"

"That's it, then," Sara proclaimed, taking the baby back from Wyatt, "we're calling her Cassie."

Angel stood to the side, while Doctor O'Hare cleaned up after the delivery, and the wolves crowded around to congratulate the new parents and coo over the new baby. It had been one of the most amazing things she'd ever experienced, and Angel was glad Sara had asked her to be a part of it. Deciding to give the newly expanded family a little space, she snuck out of the bedroom, heading for some of the snacks in the kitchen. Once presented with food, her stomach growled loudly, reminding her she'd been up for several hours without eating. Grabbing a sandwich, a cookie, and a glass of juice, Angel sat down at the kitchen table and had breakfast. Ryan and Caleb joined her about 10 minutes later, also grabbing some food. No one spoke, though Ryan kept casting glances between Angel and his brother, like he expected them to jump each other again. Angel just ignored him. Harder to ignore was what had happened out on the patio.

Despite her best efforts, Angel hadn't managed to convince Caleb she wasn't interested in him. In fact, she'd probably managed to convince him of the exact opposite. If she was being honest with herself, Angel actually regretted Ryan's interruption. Having sex with Caleb was, at the moment, both the best and worst idea Angel had ever had. The best because she was pretty sure it would be the best experience of her adult life and appease her wolf. The worst because she knew it would lead to disaster. Finishing up her meal, Angel took her dishes to the kitchen and rinsed them off before loading them into the dishwasher. She then headed to the bedroom, intending to say goodbye to Sara before leaving the compound. When she walked in,

Sara and Wyatt were laying on the bed, Cassie cradled gently in Sara's arms.

"Hey there, Mom and Dad," Angel teased, and both their faces lit up in wide grins. "How's she doing?"

"Wonderful," Wyatt replied. "Thank you, Angel, for your help during the delivery."

"Don't worry about it," Angel told him, "I'm just glad I could help."

"Do you want to hold her?" Sara asked.

Angel had no idea why, but that simple question scared the crap out of her. She'd never really been around babies, so she had no idea how to deal with them. An image of herself dropping the tiny little baby on her head suddenly flashed through Angel's mind.

"Uh, no, I'm good," Angel replied.

"Oh, come on," Sara pleaded, "you'll be fine. Come on, come sit next to me." Sara patted the bed next to her, and Angel begrudgingly came to sit on the bed. "Now," Sara explained, shifting the baby's weight in her arms so she could pass her to Angel, "just remember to support her head, okay?"

"Okay," Angel replied meekly, panicking a little as she took the small child in her arms.

Following Sara's instructions, she made sure Cassie's head rested in the crook of her elbow. Looking down, Angel saw the baby was awake, staring up at her with wide eyes. She smelled fresh and new, with a hint of wildness to her Angel recognized as her wolf - not quite ready to make an appearance yet, but waiting quietly in the background.

"This isn't so hard," Angel mumbled, mostly to herself.

"Wow," Ryan commented from the doorway, "I think we've finally found something the little witch can't handle. You can take on psycho wolves and black witches, but you're scared of babies?"

"Shut up, Ryan," Sara scolded her brother before turning back to Angel. "Don't listen to him, Angel, you're doing great."

"She looks like a deer in headlights," Caleb quipped.

"Might as well ask her now, Sara. I don't think you're ever gonna get a better chance."

"Ask me what?" Angel asked, suddenly wary.

"Wyatt and I were talking," Sara began, "and we were wondering if maybe you would be Cassie's godmother?"

The request blew Angel away; never in a million years would she have expected this. Her knee-jerk reaction was to say no, but looking down at the little girl in her arms, she knew she couldn't.

"Are you sure about this?" Angel asked. "I mean, shouldn't her godmother be a pack member?"

"Heck, no," Sara exclaimed. "None of those bitches deserve to be Cassie's godmother; most of them only pretend to be my friend so they can get closer to my brothers."

"Okay," Angel replied hesitantly, "if it's really what you want, I'll do it."

Sara squealed with delight and hugged Angel as best she could while still holding the baby.

Angel was finally able to escape around 8am. First, Sara had insisted she hold the baby for a while longer, "to get used to it," she claimed, but Angel was pretty sure they all just enjoyed seeing her out of her element. Eventually, Cassie got fussy, and Angel managed to hand her back to her mother. Caleb and Ryan then announced they were making a proper breakfast, and Angel got roped into helping.

Wyatt and Sara managed to get the baby to sleep, right after her first feeding, and Wyatt carried his Mate out to the kitchen, setting her gently at the head of the table. Everyone was quiet as they worked through piles of bacon, eggs, sausage, pancakes, and toast. Angel had to admit, it was a lot better than the breakfast she would have made herself at home.

After the table was cleared and dishes were done, Wyatt and Sara retired to their room, looking to get a little sleep. Ryan bid Angel farewell, saying he had some work to take care of, but she was pretty sure he was just trying to leave her and Caleb alone. Surprisingly, Caleb didn't try to make her stay. He offered to walk her to her car, chatting amicably with her along the way about silly little things like the weather. Even when they reached her car, he simply held the door open for her, closed it when she'd climbed in, and waved as she drove down the driveway. It left her completely baffled, and she wasn't sure if she should be relieved or worried.

Caleb could sense Angel's confusion as he walked her to her car and sent her on her way. She'd expected him to try and stop her, to try and finish what they'd started on the patio. But now that Caleb knew she wanted him – and badly – he could be patient. He strode into his office, and Ryan looked up from playing his video game, clearly confused.

"Where's Angel?" he asked.

"On her way home," Caleb replied, sitting behind his desk and booting up his computer.

"You let her leave?" Ryan asked incredulously.

"Yep."

"You've been pining over her for months, and you finally get her not only talking to you, but practically ripping your clothes off – and you just let her leave?"

"Yep."

"Why the hell would you do that?"

"Because," Caleb explained matter-of-factly, "I have a plan."

"You have a plan?" Ryan exclaimed. "What plan could possibly be better than 'throw her over your shoulder, lock her in your room, and stay there until neither of you can walk straight?'"

"Don't worry about it, Ryan," Caleb assured him. "I know what I'm doing."

"Yeah, right," Ryan scoffed. "Just don't come crying to me when your grand plan fails and she won't answer your calls again. I'm going for a run."

"Have fun," Caleb called after his brother.

Grabbing the mouse, Caleb clicked to open a browser, bringing up his email. Flipping through a pile of folders on his desk, he pulled out the one he was looking for; the label read "Alpha Conference." In his email, he brought up a saved conversation, starting a new message.

I think I have a potential solution to our problem. Remember that witch I told you about? She works well with wolves and should be able to fill the gaps in your security quite well. I'll bring her along, and you can decide for yourself if you'd like her to help out.

Regards, Caleb

Feeling quite satisfied with himself, Caleb hit the send button. Too awake to consider going to bed, he stayed in his office, working through some paperwork that had piled up recently. After working for about an hour, he was pleasantly surprised to see he already had a response to his message. Clicking it open, he read quickly, pleased with what he saw.

Sounds good. Looking forward to meeting her.
Jonathan Pike,
Master Alpha,
North America

CHAPTER 8

Alice was hungry. She stumbled down the sidewalk, the usually weak streetlights blazing so bright, they hurt her eyes. She was trying to get away from her captors and found herself in a dark alley. She leaned against the wall and tried to collect her thoughts. She'd been walking home after work. It had been late. Someone had knocked her down. Then pain. She'd woken up in some dirty warehouse. Her shirt was covered in blood. And others were there - two people covered in blood, cold and unmoving. Dead. She'd run, intent on finding help. But as she walked, her hunger grew stronger. It was like she hadn't eaten in days.

A dumpster was only a few feet away. She shuffled towards it and lifted the lid. The smell almost overpowered her, but she noticed a pizza box and grabbed it, letting the dumpster lid fall shut with a loud bang. She heard something move inside the box and opened it, finding several half-eaten crusts. She grabbed them and shoved them into her mouth, practically inhaling the stale hunks of bread. But just as soon as she'd swallowed them, her stomach revolted, and she bent over, heaving uncontrollably. She emptied her stomach completely. The hunger was still there.

"What's wrong with me?" she said to herself.

"That's not the kind of food you want."

She glanced up and saw two men approaching her, moving slowly and carefully, like they knew she might run. Under normal circumstances, she would have. But something stopped her.

"What do you mean?" Her voice trembled, sounding like a shout when she'd intended to whisper.

"Come with us," one of them said, "and we'll show you."

Something unseen tugged at her when he said that, and she found her feet moving of their own accord.

"Come with us," he repeated, "and everything will be OK."

Alice had the distinct impression nothing was going to be OK, but she found herself unable to resist as they led her back the way she'd come. Back to the warehouse with the dead people.

CHAPTER 9

Angel wasn't sure what confused her most, the fact that Caleb had just let her leave the compound, or that he'd stopped calling her. A small part of her thought maybe, just maybe it had all been an ego thing for him. That he'd been so persistent because he couldn't accept the fact that a woman would refuse him. And now that he knew she was attracted to him, he didn't need or want anything more from her. Even her wolf thought the idea was a little ridiculous. Male wolves - especially Alphas - were known for having sensitive egos, but Caleb wasn't a complete jerk. Unfortunately, when Wednesday rolled around and she still hadn't heard a thing from him, Angel was a wreck.

"Fuck!" she cursed, hurling her phone across the room after checking it for the umpteenth time that day and seeing no messages or missed calls.

Wasn't this what she'd wanted? For Caleb to give up on her? It had been one thing to hope for it, but now that it had happened, Angel was torn. Her wolf was pissed, convinced her human half had somehow really managed to fuck things up with their Mate.

Retrieving the phone from the floor, Angel pulled up her list of contacts. She paused at Caleb's number, wanting so badly to call him, but she knew she shouldn't. Scrolling down, she came to Sara's number, stabbing the "Call" button and holding the phone to her ear. Taking a few deep breaths, Angel tried to calm herself as the phone rang. Sara picked up on the third ring.

"Hello, Angel!" Sara greeted her brightly. "How are you?"

"I'm good," Angel replied. "How are you? And how's Cassie?"

"We're all great," Sara gushed. "She's such a happy baby, and you should see Wyatt and my brothers with her - they're naturals at this stuff!"

"That's great," Angel said, an image of Caleb holding a baby in his arms flashing through her mind, causing her heart to clench painfully. Angel had never wanted kids, but apparently meeting your Mate could change a lot of things. Forcing away those unwanted thoughts, it took her a moment to realize Sara had asked her a question. "Uh, sorry," she apologized, "say that again?"

"I asked if you wanted to grab lunch," Sara repeated. "Wyatt and the boys offered to watch Cassie for a few hours so I could get out of the house."

"Sure," Angel replied, "where do you want to go?"

"How about Bobby's?" Sara suggested. "I feel like something deep fried."

"Sounds great. Meet you there in thirty minutes?"

"Deal, see you soon!"

Angel hung up the phone, feeling a little better. Maybe Caleb has just been really busy with the new baby, and that's why he hadn't called. Hopefully, she'd be able to get more information from Sara at lunch, without actually asking her outright. Sighing deeply, Angel tore through the house, finding something clean to wear before gathering up her purse and keys and heading out the door.

Bobby's was an average-looking sports bar in downtown Waterloo. It was typically more popular with college students and during sports games, so at 1pm on a Wednesday, there were plenty of empty tables. Angel arrived first, grabbing a booth and watching the door for Sara. The she-wolf arrived about ten minutes later, spotting Angel quickly and joining her at the table.

"Hey!" Sara exclaimed, sliding into the seat across from Angel. "This is fun, I haven't been out without Wyatt or one of my brothers in ages."

"You were pregnant," Angel remarked, grinning when Sara stuck her tongue out at her.

"That's what they said," Sara complained. The waitress arrived a moment later, taking their drink orders and leaving them some time to browse the menus. "What are you getting?" Sara asked.

"Definitely the burger," Angel replied, "it's pretty good."

"Ooh, sounds yummy. I think I'll get one, too. And maybe some mozzarella sticks."

They debated the different appetizers for a minute or so, finally deciding on mozzarella sticks and garlic bread. The waitress arrived with their drinks, took their meal orders and headed off to the kitchen.

"So," Sara began casually, "what's this I hear about you and Caleb going at it on the patio the other day?"

Angel's face flushed red, and she lowered her head to the tabletop, groaning out loud.

"Oh, God," Angel replied. "I'm guessing Ryan told you about that?"

"Yep." Sara grinned, patting her gently on the shoulder. "Don't worry about it, that kind of thing is pretty normal with wolves."

"But it shouldn't have happened," Angel said. "I was there for you, and Caleb and I...it just wouldn't work."

"Why not?" Sara asked. "And don't tell me 'it's complicated.' That's a crappy answer, and you know it." When Angel hesitated, Sara reached out and took her hand. "Do you like Caleb?"

"Yes."

"And I know for sure he likes you, so what's the problem? Is it because he's a wolf?"

"No!" Angel exclaimed. "It's not. Definitely not."

"Then what is it? I swear I won't tell Caleb - not a word."

Angel struggled to come up with an explanation close enough to the truth without actually revealing her secret.

"I have trust issues," Angel explained, "and it's easier to

just bail on any kind of relationship before things get serious. And I know Caleb and I aren't anything right now, let alone anything serious, but I've never felt so strongly about anyone before. It scares the crap out of me."

"So now I know two things that scare you," Sara teased, "babies and relationships."

"I am not afraid of babies," Angel insisted. "I've just never been around one before. And she was just so small, I was afraid I'd drop her or something."

"Wolves have hard heads, even as babies," Sara replied, "not that I think you would ever drop Cassie."

The waitress arrived with their appetizers, and they both fell silent for a few minutes, munching on the greasy snacks. Despite the fact that she'd avoided discussing Caleb with Sara for months, she was glad they were talking now. It was somehow freeing to admit she was scared of her feelings for Caleb, even if she wasn't being completely honest. Angel trusted Sara - more than anyone else, actually - but she had no idea how the she-wolf would react to the revelation that Angel was a hybrid. Or whether she'd be able to keep that information to herself.

"So," Sara continued when they'd demolished the appetizers, "what are you going to do now?"

"No idea," Angel answered honestly. "I don't even know if Caleb is even interested anymore; he hasn't called me all week."

"He hasn't?" Sara asked, looking surprised.

"Nope, not even a text. And the other day when I said I was leaving, he didn't say a word. He just walked me to my car and waved as I drove away."

"Huh," Sara replied, deep in thought. "That's strange."

"Whatever," Angel said, trying to sound like she didn't care. "Maybe he's not interested anymore. It's not a big deal. I'll get over it."

"Oh, no," Sara insisted, "he's definitely still interested. The only thing that would explain his change of behavior is that he has a plan in the works."

"A plan?" Angel asked, slightly worried.

Sara laughed at her, reassuringly patting her hand.

"Welcome to dealing with an Alpha," she replied. "They're always up for a challenge."

"Awesome," Angel grumbled as the waitress arrived with their meals.

The burgers were massive, covered in cheese and bacon, and rare, just how she liked them. They dug into their food, continuing to chat about random things - the weather, cute things Cassie had done - but never returning to their discussion about Caleb. Angel was grateful for that; Sara had given her a lot to think about.

Before too long, their plates were cleaned, and the waitress came by to clear the table. Declining dessert, they paid the bill and headed out to the parking lot. Angel walked Sara to her car, knowing Wyatt would appreciate the gesture, and gave the taller woman a big hug.

"I had fun today," Angel said, "thanks for inviting me out."

"Don't mention it," Sara told her, "I had fun, too. We should have a girls night sometime soon."

"Okay," Angel agreed.

Sara pulled her keys from her purse and unlocked her door, turning to Angel before she climbed into the car.

"Sometimes things are scary, but they're worth it," Sara told her. "Think about it, you might be pleasantly surprised."

Angel felt a lot better after lunch with Sara. She was incredibly relieved to know Caleb hadn't completely given up on her, but a little worried about what he was planning. Wednesday afternoon, she went for a long run, working out the last bit of tension that had built up from worrying over the last few days. Trying to stay busy, she cleaned her house from top to bottom, reorganized her files from work, and did some baking. It was late Thursday afternoon by the time Angel remembered she had a check-in at work the next day. The appointment loomed before her, ruining her good mood. While each check-in revealed a reduction in the extra power she'd gained from the blood magic, the Agency wasn't happy with how slowly the magic was leaving her system.

Ignoring the fact that she was bored out of her mind most days, Angel had no idea what she'd do if she wasn't able to go back to work. Being an Agent was all she'd ever known. She loved her job, and it was the one place in her life where she always knew exactly what she was doing. Trying to dispel those negative thoughts, Angel grabbed a plate of cookies and turned on the TV, flipping to her favorite movie channel.

CHAPTER 10

Angel climbed out of bed Friday morning, already in a bad mood. Showering quickly, she pulled on a pair of jeans and nice top, grabbed a quick breakfast, and headed out the door. The drive into the city was busier than she was used to, mostly because it was later in the morning. But her appointment wasn't until 11am, and she sure as hell wasn't going to hang around the office any longer than necessary.

She pulled into the parking garage, spent way too much time trying to find a parking spot, then headed for the elevator – but before she reached it, a familiar voice called her name.

"Angel!"

She turned and smiled despite her circumstances when she saw her boss headed her way.

"Director Bates. It's good to see you."

"I'm glad I caught you, Angel," he said, leading her towards a section of the garage further from the elevators. "I wanted to see how you were doing."

"Dying of boredom," she replied, "but otherwise fine. How about you?"

Angel had heard enough to know Bates wasn't on probation and hadn't lost his job, but the rest of the details weren't publicly available. While he hadn't been the one to perform the blood magic, he'd not only allowed it to happen and he'd acted as a donor. Scott, being a Warner with plenty of connections, had come out completely unscathed. She didn't begrudge him that; he had the potential to be a great Agent and didn't deserve to have his career tanked alongside Angel.

Bates absently waved his hand.

"I've been around long enough to collect a few favors, and

I'm not usually one to rock the boat. I got a slap on the wrist and a stern look. I do wish I'd been able to do more to help your case, though."

Angel just shrugged.

"They didn't fire me outright. Or lock me up. Probation makes sense. I just wish it wasn't dragging on so long, or that they'd give me more information about my test results. Being in the dark sucks."

"Unfortunately, I can't help much with that either. They keep that information locked up pretty tight. But I'm confident you'll be back to work soon enough."

"Thanks."

"You should go," Bates said, "before I make you late."

She frowned but started heading back towards the elevator. They climbed in, and she hit the button for the third floor. When they reached her stop, Angel stepped out, giving Bates a little wave.

"Bye."

"Good luck," he replied as the elevator doors closed.

Angel turned and headed towards the front desk, where she was greeted by the usual dreary secretary and directed to sign the visitors log, then wait in the sitting area to the left. Flopping down into a well-worn armchair, Angel tried not to fidget. About ten minutes later, a woman entered the lobby, calling out Angel's name.

"That's me," Angel replied, standing quickly.

"Come with me, please," the older woman instructed.

Angel followed her down a familiar hallway and into one of the test rooms. Most of the time, these rooms were used to gauge the magical abilities of potential Agents. Angel wasn't entirely sure how the tests worked, but basically they ran you through a series of spells, changing up the situation every now and then, and somehow they were able to get a good idea of your power level.

"Have a seat, Miss Myers," she instructed. "You'll receive instructions shortly, and then the test will begin."

Angel frowned, annoyed that the woman had called her "Miss" instead of "Agent," but before she could say anything, she was gone. The room contained a small table with a speaker box on it and a chair. The opposite wall showed Angel her reflection, but she knew from past experience it was a two-way mirror. Several witches sat behind the glass and conducted the test, delivering instructions through the speaker box. Various sensors and cameras placed throughout the room relayed various pieces of information to the witches behind the glass. The room was insulated against outside magic, which made the readings more accurate and prevented cheating.

"Are you ready, Agent Myers?" a male voice asked through the speaker box.

"Yes," Angel replied.

"Then let us begin."

Three hours later, Angel had completed the magical tests and moved on to the psychological evaluation part of her check-in. Doctor Weaver was an older witch, with more grey hairs than not, and for some reason he really got on Angel's nerves. Every time she saw him, he would ask seemingly random questions, listen to her answer, and scribble notes down on his clipboard. This repeated ad nauseum until their time was up. Today wasn't any different.

"Did you have any pets growing up?" Doctor Weaver asked.

"I had a goldfish when I was six," Angel replied. "His name was Goldie, and he died when I overfed him. We flushed him down the toilet."

Scribble, scribble, scribble.

"No other pets? A cat, or a dog maybe?"

"Nope."

"Why not?"

"My mother didn't want them," Angel explained, letting her frustration show.

"Is everything alright?" the doctor asked, pen poised

above his clipboard.

"No," Angel admitted, "everything is not alright. I want to get back to work. I've done the tests, I've proven I'm not performing any more blood rites, and I've jumped through all the damn hoops you people put in front of me. What else do I have to do before I can get back to my job?"

"Well," the doctor began, and Angel knew she wasn't going to like his answer, "you have certainly complied with all the requirements of your probation, and your test results don't indicate any abnormal power fluctuations. Unfortunately, we're just not quite ready to sign off on your return to the field."

"Why not?" Angel demanded.

"We're concerned the stress of the job might lead you astray," Weaver explained.

"Lead me astray!?" Angel exclaimed. "You mean you're worried I'll use blood magic once I'm back on the job because it's easier?"

"Correct."

"In case you haven't noticed, Doctor, I'm not one to take the easy route. I worked hard for everything I've achieved, I earned it. I became an Agent because I want to help people, and you think I might start killing people?"

"That's not what I said," Weaver tried to explain, but Angel had heard enough.

"Are we done?"

"We do have another ten minutes," Doctor Weaver told her.

"Do you have any more questions for me?"

"No, not at the moment."

"Excellent. Goodbye."

Grabbing her coat, Angel stormed from the room and down the hallway. She reached the lobby, where a witch waited with a clipboard.

"The Agency will inform you of any changes to your probation within three business days, Miss Myers," she explained, then held up the clipboard. "Please sign here."

"Yeah, fine, whatever," Angel muttered, quickly signing her name.

Stepping into the elevator, she resisted the urge to punch something, viciously stabbing the button for the parking garage. The elevator seemed to move at a crawl, and Angel was immensely grateful when it let her out at the parking level without stopping at any of the floors in-between. Climbing into her car, she flew out of the garage, heading towards home. She grumbled to herself the whole drive, upset and frustrated. She'd done everything right, played nice with the tests, and the doctor and all those stupid office witches who looked at her funny every time she walked in the door.

Pulling into her driveway, she jerked to a stop, turned off the car, and climbed out, slamming the door behind her.

"Stupid fucking doctor," Angel muttered to herself, "thinks he know everything. Tell me this, Doctor - what the fuck does my having a goldfish instead of a cat have to do with me getting my damn job back? Huh? Tell me that!"

Deciding she needed a nice, relaxing shower, Angel stormed inside, dumped her purse on the ground, and headed for her bedroom. She kicked off her shoes, unbuckled her belt, and pushed her jeans down her legs. Her pants were around her ankles by the time she realized something was amiss. She turned back towards the living room, her mind taking a moment to process what she was seeing. Caleb, Ryan, and Wyatt were in the kitchen, Scott and Sara sat at the kitchen table, and Cassie sat happily in her mother's lap.

"Uh," Angel began, trying to find the right words.

"Surprise!" Sara exclaimed, grinning widely.

"Nice undies," Ryan said, winking at her.

"Shit!" Angel cursed, realizing she was standing there with her pants down. She quickly pulled them back up, then pulled herself together enough to speak. "What are all of you doing here?"

"We wanted to surprise you with Thanksgiving dinner," Sara explained. "Scott told Ryan you had a check-in with work today, so we snuck in after you left to get everything ready."

Angel went from pissed off to completely overwhelmed faster than she could track. Pausing a moment to take it all in, she saw a fully cooked turkey sitting on the counter, ready to be carved. Wyatt was mashing a giant pot of potatoes, Ryan was draining a pot of carrots, and Caleb was scooping stuffing out of the turkey. She couldn't believe they'd gone to such lengths to surprise her like this.

"Wow," Angel said, failing to come up with a better way to express herself. "Just, wow. This is amazing, I can't believe you did all this for me."

"Don't be silly," Sara told her, "you're our friend, and you've done so much for us, we just wanted to give a little back. Now come on, have some wine and relax, the boys are almost done with dinner."

Angel moved to sit with Sara, still a little shell-shocked. Taking the glass of wine Scott offered her, she took a big swallow.

"How on Earth did you get roped into this, Scott?" she asked, curious because she was pretty sure the kid was still terrified of wolves.

"Ryan's been teaching me how to fight," Scott explained, "and he mentioned they were looking for a way to surprise you with something nice, so I told them you were going to be out today."

"What?!" Angel spluttered, having just taken a sip of wine. "What do you mean, Ryan's teaching you how to fight?"

"Relax, Angel," Ryan said, "I'm going easy on him."

"I thought you were afraid of wolves?" Angel asked Scott.

"I am...I mean, I was," Scott replied, "but most of them are pretty nice."

"I'm guessing your brother has no clue?"

"Uh, no," Scott admitted, "and I'm planning on keeping it that way. He's not a big fan of wolves."

"Or me, for that matter," Angel added. Scott laughed nervously, and Angel patted him on the back. "Don't worry about it, Scott," she told him. "Just make sure he doesn't find out you're hanging out with us."

"Deal," Scott agreed.

"Looks like we're just about ready," Caleb announced from the kitchen.

A moment later, Ryan and Wyatt came and set several bowls full of food on the table. Caleb followed, carrying the very large turkey, which he set in the center of the table. Sara stood and placed Cassie gently in her car seat, positioning it on the sofa so she could watch the baby while she ate. Angel took a seat next to Sara, with Caleb on her other side.

"Alright," Caleb said, holding up the carving knife and fork, "who wants a leg?"

CHAPTER 11

Thanksgiving dinner with the wolves was incredible. Angel had never seen so much food in her life; she was in heaven. After turkey and stuffing, Sara dragged Wyatt into the kitchen, and they returned with no fewer than seven pies. After gorging herself, Angel sat back in her chair with a glass of wine.

"That was probably the best Thanksgiving meal I've ever had," she said. "Thank you, all of you, this was a wonderful surprise."

"Don't mention it," Ryan told her, gathering up plates and heading into the kitchen.

"Let me help," Angel said, collecting empty glasses and cutlery.

"No, no, no," Sara scolded, taking the dishes from Angel's hands. "We'll clean everything up. You go watch Cassie."

"Are you sure?" Angel asked. "I mean, you guys did all the cooking."

"Positive," Sara grinned, pushing her into the living room. "Now go spend some time with your goddaughter."

"Okay, okay," Angel relented, moving to sit on the sofa next to Cassie's car seat. The little girl was wide awake and stared up at Angel curiously. "Hello there, little one," Angel cooed, brushing her fingers against the baby's tiny little hand. Cassie latched on to her finger with a surprisingly strong grip, gurgling happily. Angel pulled slightly, trying to disengage the infant, but Cassie held on tight.

"Here," Caleb offered, sitting on the other side of the car seat and holding up a small stuffed bear, "she likes this one."

He held the toy out to Cassie, who released Angel's finger and grabbed at the teddy bear instead. Angel smiled as Cassie immediately stuffed one of the bear's feet into her mouth.

"She's definitely a wolf," Angel joked, bopping Cassie on the nose and making the girl grin.

"So," Caleb began, and Angel was a little worried about what he'd say next, "I take it the check-in didn't go well?"

"No, not really," Angel replied, relieved and disappointed at the same time. "The tests confirm the power I gained from the blood magic is fading, but it's not fading as quickly as they'd like."

"They don't think you're going out and getting more, do they?" Caleb asked, concerned.

"No," Angel assured him, "that would show up on the tests pretty clearly. I think it's the stupid shrink they've got me seeing that's the problem."

"Why does it not surprise me you don't like a psychiatrist?" Caleb teased.

"Psychologist," Angel corrected. "And if you had to sit in a room with him for an hour, answering stupid questions that are totally irrelevant, you'd hate him, too."

"Don't worry," Caleb told her, "I'm sure you'll be back to work soon."

"But will I go crazy from boredom in the meantime?" Angel asked, making him laugh. It was a nice sound, and she realized how nice it was to spend time with him, how natural it was.

"I can't answer that for you," Caleb replied, "but I might be able to help."

"Oh?" Angel asked. She was trying to sound calm, but internally her wolf was throwing up images of the different ways he could keep her busy.

"I might have a job for you," he continued. "There's a conference in one week in Barrie. Every Alpha in North America is invited, and the Master Alpha is looking for a little extra security. I recommended you, and he liked the idea. If you're interested, he'll pay your way, you can meet him, and he can decide if he wants to hire you for the week."

Angel's heart fell, but she managed to pull herself together before he noticed.

"You think me working security at a werewolf conference is a good idea?" she asked. "You really think any of them would even listen to me?"

"You'd be on the Master Alpha's private security detail," Caleb explained. "Your interactions with other wolves would be limited."

"Oh," Angel said, surprised. "That's one hell of a recommendation."

Caleb shrugged. "I've worked with the Master Alpha a lot in the past. He values my opinion."

"Why do I feel like there's more to this than basic security?" Angel asked, her wolf telling her Caleb was leaving something out.

Caleb smiled apologetically. "There is," he told her, "but I'm not allowed to discuss it right now. The Master Alpha will explain everything once we get to Barrie, and if you're not interested, there'll be no hard feelings."

Instinct told Angel this was a bad idea; whether it was the details Caleb wasn't allowed to share or the fact that she'd potentially be close to him for a whole week, she wasn't sure. She considered the idea for a moment, but ultimately her curiosity, and the desire to finally do something after months off the job, won out.

"Alright," she told him, "I'm in."

CHAPTER 12

Angel was a bundle of nerves for the next week. She was both terrified and elated to spend so much time around Caleb. On the one hand, there was the ever-present fear that he'd find out what she was and reject her, Mate or not. On the other hand, Angel was allowing herself to believe maybe, just maybe they could find a way to make things work. Maybe.

With that in mind, she flipped between incredibly depressed and overly optimistic a few times a day. During her depressed moments, she convinced herself Caleb had completely given up on her and recommending her for this job was his way of putting her firmly into the friend category. Or she imagined the worst possible reactions he could have to finding out she was a hybrid. Top of the list was him selling her to the highest bidder. During her optimistic moments, she flounced around her house like a twelve-year-old girl with a crush, fiddling with her hair and grinning like an idiot whenever she passed a mirror.

It was three days before the conference when Angel finally realized she was about to be thrown head first into a very delicate situation. Dominant wolves didn't get along well on principle, mostly because their instincts pushed them to determine who the most dominant male was, usually by fighting. Every Alpha in North America was invited to the conference - 127 in total - and each Alpha could bring up to three additional wolves with them, for a total of over 400 werewolves. Angel was starting to get a little worried that throwing a witch into that mix would end badly. She voiced her concerns when Caleb called that evening to figure out travel plans.

"Are you sure this is a good idea, Caleb?" she asked. "I mean, I get along fine with your wolves, most of the time, but most wolves really don't like witches."

"It'll be fine, Angel," Caleb reassured her. "You've been invited by the Master Alpha. Anyone who disagrees with his choice in security would have to challenge him openly, and no one's going to do that."

"Alright," Angel relented, "but if things get stupid - between the wolves, at least - I'm out of there."

"Definitely," Caleb agreed. "So I figured it would be easier if we drove up together on Sunday. Then we can check into the hotel, meet with the Master Alpha, and get a good night's sleep before the conference starts. What do you think?"

"Works for me," Angel replied, trying to sound calm, even though the idea of being trapped in a car with him for two hours was a little scary. "My car or yours?"

"Mine, if that's okay," Caleb said. "I've got some extra stuff I need to bring, and I don't think it'll all fit in your car."

"Okay, pick me up at about eleven?"

"Perfect, see you then. Call me if you have any more questions."

"Will do."

"Goodnight."

"'Night."

Angel hit the "End Call" button on her phone and resisted the urge both to jump up and down and throw up. It was going to be a very interesting week. Taking a deep breath to calm herself, Angel set down the phone and decided it was a good time for a run.

CHAPTER 13

"Stay here. Stay quiet."

Alice stayed. She had no other option; she couldn't disobey, and on the few occasions they hadn't explicitly told her to stay put and she'd tried to run, they'd found her easily. Besides, there was nowhere for her to go. Not after what she'd done. Not after what she'd become.

Others were there with her. Others like her. The man next to her had been an addict living on the street. She spotted a woman named Mary, who'd been a waitress at a twenty-four hour diner. They talked when they were left alone, and they all had the same story. They'd been out at night when they were attacked. When they woke up, they were different.

The people in charge kept them secluded in basements, shipping containers, sometimes even sewers. They brought them food - Alice shuddered at the thought even as her mouth watered - but they still had no idea why they were there. What their captors actually wanted from them. Then last night everyone had been loaded into a transport truck and driven for hours. Now they were in a large warehouse, and more people were arriving by the hour. She had no idea what was going on. No one did.

Another truck arrived, and as the doors opened, Alice was nearly overwhelmed by the smell. Death. That's what her overly sensitive nose told her, which was why she was surprised when people started shambling out of the truck. No, not people. These creatures couldn't possibly be people. They moved awkwardly, like they were drunk or sick. They didn't make a sound, didn't look around. They shuffled towards the corner they were directed to and just stopped dead. The truck pulled away, and still they didn't move. Most of them were just facing the wall, but there were a few whose faces she could see, and what she saw was unsettling. Blank, vacant stares set into pale faces. Whatever had been done to these people, there was nothing left of who they had been.

CHAPTER 14

Sunday morning dawned bright and chilly. Angel was up early, mostly because she'd been unable to sleep very well. She went for a quick run, showered, ate, then spent two hours figuring out what to pack. Her suitcase and almost every piece of clothing she owned was laid out on her bed. At first she'd tried to pack just work clothes, then she realized maybe she wouldn't need her leather pants and vest, so she pulled out everything and threw in jeans and T-shirts. Then she started worrying about what Caleb would think of her clothes, so she threw in some pretty blouses and a pair of dress pants; and then she thought he'd realize she was dressing differently and figure she was up to something.

Ripping everything out of her suitcase, Angel started over. After a little more deliberation, she decided to bring one set of her usual work clothes, just in case, a couple pairs of jeans, some T-shirts, and a few nicer looking outfits in case she was expected to dress up for the job. Her utility belt went in as well, though it was lacking a few key components. Her handcuffs had been confiscated, as well as the healing potions she was used to; they were reserved for use in law enforcement and hospitals and weren't available to the general public. In their place, Angel had bought a half-dozen vials of the strongest publicly available healing potion she could find. It was still about half as effective as the ones from work, but since she was a hybrid, Angel figured she could manage. She'd been able to keep her gun, but her badge had also been confiscated.

When she was finally happy with what she'd packed - or at least as happy as she could be - Angel hauled her stuff out of her room and piled it in front of the door. Looking to kill time before Caleb showed up, she tidied her room, washed the dishes, and cleaned out her fridge so she wouldn't come back to anything unpleasant. She was just finishing up when she heard a vehicle approaching the house.

Caleb drove up in a large black SUV with tinted windows, put the vehicle in park, cut the engine, and hopped out. He was wearing jeans, with a flannel shirt over a black tee, and he looked really good. Angel took a few moments to admire the way he moved as he approached the house. He was wearing dark sunglasses, and the sun reflected off his blond hair. Her wolf growled in approval as Caleb reached the front door, and Angel took a deep breath, trying to maintain control. A knock came on the door, and Caleb opened it a moment later. Removing his sunglasses as he stepped inside, his eyes found hers, and he grinned.

"Ready to go?" he asked.

"Yeah," Angel replied, "just finishing up here."

Caleb gestured to the suitcase and backpack at the front door. "Can I take these out to the truck?"

"Yeah," Angel replied, "thanks! I'll be out in a minute."

"No problem," Caleb told her, scooping up her bags and heading outside.

Angel took another deep breath to calm herself, finished cleaning the last dirty dish, and pulled the sink stopper. She pulled on her shoes, grabbed her jacket, purse, and keys, then turned to survey the room. She knew by the time she came home again, things would likely have changed, and drastically.

"Well," she whispered to herself, "here goes nothing."

The drive began in silence, but Angel really didn't mind. She was worried if they did start getting chatty, Caleb might take advantage of the fact that she couldn't go anywhere and start asking her questions she still wasn't ready to answer. They drove towards Waterloo, picking up the highway as soon as they could. The beast of a vehicle drove surprisingly smoothly, and Angel found herself playing with all the neat toys it had built into the dashboard. Turning on the built-in satellite radio, she searched the channels for something she liked. One channel spewed horrible rap music that hurt her sensitive ears, another was kiddie pop, and yet another was Christian rock. Continuing to search, she finally found a decent channel. Johnny Cash flowed into the cabin of the SUV, and Angel found herself drumming on her thighs along with the music.

"Country fan?" Caleb asked.

"Heck, yes," Angel replied. "Johnny Cash is especially awesome. How about you?"

"Country is definitely one of my favorites," Caleb told her, "but I could never get into Cash. He's a little depressing."

"Maybe," Angel admitted, "but I don't think his voice would work for happy songs."

"Fair enough."

"So," Angel began, "you left Ryan in charge while you're gone, I assume?"

"Yep."

"You sure he's not going to throw some wild party and burn the house down?"

Caleb laughed. "Nah," he said, "Sara wouldn't let him. Besides, he won't have that much free time. I made sure to leave him lots of work to keep him occupied."

"I kinda wish I had siblings," Angel said thoughtfully. "It was kinda lonely growing up."

"They have their good moments and their bad," Caleb told her, "but in the end, I wouldn't give them up for the world. Even Ryan."

Angel grinned at him, then fell silent. They drove in silence for a bit, and she could tell Caleb wanted to ask her something. Eventually, he managed to spit it out.

"So, where's your dad?" he asked.

"Not a clue," Angel told him matter-of-factly.

Caleb held up a hand. "I'm sorry," he said, "I shouldn't have asked. It's not my business."

"No," Angel reassured him, "don't worry about it, it's a fair question. My mom was attacked, and she got pregnant, but she decided to keep me. As far as I know, she never figured out who the guy was, not that she was really interested."

"Oh," Caleb said, clearly not expecting that response. "I'm so sorry."

"Don't be," Angel told him, "it's not like it really affected me all that much. My mom might be a little crazy, but she loves me, and she did a great job raising me on her own."

"That she did," Caleb agreed.

Angel blushed slightly at the compliment, then fiddled with the temperature controls in an attempt to distract herself. Cooped up in a vehicle with Caleb, his scent surrounded her, and for once it didn't make her edgy. Her wolf seemed content just to sit back and enjoy the ride, perhaps because she sensed her human half was starting to see reason. Angel had to admit, she was starting to think it might be worth the risk to just tell Caleb the truth. Even if he didn't want to be with her, knowing the potential risks, at least then she (and her wolf) might be able to move on. Angel never really had imagined a happily-ever-after scenario for herself. No dreams of a white wedding, or even children for that matter. Her fear had always held her back. She wasn't about to start hoping for a future with Caleb just yet, but this was probably as good a chance as she was ever going to get, so maybe she should at least give it a try.

Settling into her seat, Angel took a deep breath, then turned to Caleb. "You ever played the alphabet game?"

CHAPTER 15

They played the alphabet game for the rest of the trip. As expected, they both got hung up on "Q" for a while, until they happened upon several signs for a toasted sub place. By the time they reached Barrie, Caleb was stuck on "U," but Angel had made it all the way to "X," making her the winner.

"On the way back," Caleb informed her as they pulled into a parking spot at the hotel, "I want a rematch."

"Deal," Angel replied, "but I'll still win."

"We'll see," Caleb told her.

They grabbed their things out of the car and headed for the lobby. Angel stacked their luggage onto a cart, while Caleb checked them in. After a few minutes chatting with the receptionist and handing over his credit card, Caleb was back, handing her a room key.

"Room 203," he told her. "They're gonna take care of our luggage, and were going to go straight up to see the Master Alpha."

"Okay," Angel replied.

After cautioning the bellhop to be careful with the bag that contained her spells and gun, they boarded the elevator. Caleb punched the button for the 4th floor, and the elevator lurched into motion.

"Anything I should know about this guy?" Angel asked Caleb as they watched the button for each floor light up as they passed.

"Just your basic werewolf stuff," Caleb told her. "He's a pretty laid back guy, a little less aggressive than most Alphas."

"That seems a little counterintuitive," Angel commented.

"You'd think so, but not really," Caleb explained. "Most Alphas gain the position because they're strong. They keep the position if they're strong and smart; it's one thing to be the strongest wolf in a pack, but if you aren't smart enough to lead, the pack won't follow you. To be Master Alpha, you have to be strong, smart, and able to recognize where each of those traits is needed. When dealing with other Alphas, a heavy hand can sometimes make things worse."

"This stuff is a lot more complicated than I thought," Angel remarked as the elevator dinged and doors opened.

They stepped out together, and Caleb guided them down the hallway to the left.

"Yep," he told her as they stopped in front of room #412, "but don't worry about it, you'll do just fine."

Caleb knocked twice, and after a few moments Angel heard movement behind the door, then the sound of the chain being removed. The door opened to reveal a very tall, very large man, with sandy brown hair and bright green eyes. He smiled when he saw Caleb and enveloped him in a big bear hug, clapping him on the back.

"Caleb," he exclaimed, "about time you got here!"

"Jesse," Caleb greeted the other wolf with similar enthusiasm, "it's been too long."

"Come in, come in," Jesse encouraged as he released Caleb and stepped back into the room.

Angel followed behind Caleb, knowing it was best to let him take the lead. Once they were inside and the door was closed, she got a good look at the room. It was a suite, with separate living and sleeping areas. They were in the living area, which had a couch, a couple chairs, and a large TV hanging on the back wall. To the left was a kitchenette with a mini-fridge, sink, and coffee pot, and to the right was a large set of double doors, currently closed, that presumably led to the bedroom. Another wolf was in the room with them; he was big and bulky, with bright red hair and a sour expression on his face as he watched her. Angel wasn't surprised that she seemed to have found another wolf who didn't like witches.

"So," Jesse began, talking to Caleb but gesturing to Angel, "this is the witch you told us about?"

"Yep," Caleb replied, "this is Angel Myers. She's the WEA Agent who took out the black witch who was giving us trouble a couple months ago. And as of a few weeks ago, she's the godmother of my niece."

"Well," Jesse whistled appreciatively, "I'm not sure which of those is most impressive; female wolves are pretty damn picky about who they let near their pups. Sara must really like you." He grinned and held out his hand. "I'm Jesse. Nice to meet you."

"It's nice to meet you," Angel told Jesse, taking the offered hand, a little surprised a wolf would initiate a handshake.

"Jesse and his father meet with a lot of humans and witches," Caleb explained. "They found it easier just to adapt and get used to handshakes instead of trying to break everyone else of the habit."

"Oh," Angel replied, "that makes sense, I suppose."

"Come on in, and have a seat," Jesse told them. "My father is just on the phone, and he'll be out in a few minutes."

Caleb flopped down on the love seat, and Angel sat next to him, while the red headed wolf continued to frown at her.

"This is Matt," Jesse introduced the other man. "Don't mind the grumpy look, he always looks like that. He's head of security for the pack, and the conference."

Angel nodded politely, and Matt grunted at her. Jesse took one of the chairs opposite them, and he and Caleb started chatting, catching up on things that had happened since they'd last talked. Angel tried her best not to feel nervous, but it was difficult with Matt giving her the stink-eye. She was really hoping the Master Alpha was as "laid back" as Caleb had said, because there was no way she was going to work there if the big boss wolf didn't want her there.

After a few minutes, the bedroom door opened. Matt went from slouching against the wall to standing up straight, and Jesse and Caleb both stood. Angel followed their example and watched as a middle-aged, rather unimpressive looking man crossed the room to join them. He was still built like a wolf - tall and muscular - but he had an air of calmness that seemed almost contagious. It seemed Jesse had inherited most of his looks from his father; the two were almost carbon copies, the major differences being the bits of grey at the older wolf's temples and fine lines on his face.

"Caleb," the Master Alpha greeted, patting the younger man on the shoulder. "How are you?"

"Doing well, Jonathan," Caleb replied, "and you?"

The Master Alpha smiled. "Doing well," he said, "but I would be doing better if Matt here would stop being so damn paranoid. If he had his way, I'd have a guard watching me while I sleep."

"What about Melanie?" Caleb suggested. "You'd have a hard time finding someone who would want to mess with her."

The Master Alpha laughed loudly. "I'll have to tell my Mate you find her so intimidating," he said. Caleb stepped back, and it was Angel's turn. "You must be Angel."

"Yes, sir," Angel replied. "It's nice to meet you."

"Please," the Master Alpha said, "call me Jonathan. Thank you for coming."

"Thanks for having me," Angel said.

"Please, why don't we sit?" Jonathan suggested, and they all reclaimed their seats. Jonathan sat in the chair next to Jesse. "So, Caleb tells me you're an Agent and you helped them take down a black witch a few months ago."

"That's right," Angel answered, "but, uh, I feel I should probably let you know I'm currently on probation."

Matt made a scoffing noise from behind Jesse.

"What for?" Jonathan asked.

"Well," Angel began, "to stop the black witch, I had to make use of legal blood magic. The Agency doesn't want me in the field until it's worked its way out of my system and they're positive there were no lasting effects."

"'Legal blood magic,'" Jonathan repeated. "I'm afraid I'm not sure how blood magic can be legal. Can you please explain?"

"Of course. Legal blood magic means you don't kill anyone or anything to get the power; the blood is given freely by donors."

"In this case," Caleb explained, "the donors were myself, Ryan, and two other WEA agents."

Jonathan nodded thoughtfully. "The black witch you were pursuing, I recall he had killed several wolves, including an Alpha's son. As I understand it, that gave him the ability to use wolf magic, which made his attacks more effective against wolves, correct?"

"Yes, that's correct," Angel replied, impressed by his knowledge of blood magic. "When the option of using legal blood magic was first suggested, we initially decided it wasn't worth the potential risk. Unfortunately, the black witch managed to take one of Caleb's wolves captive, and blood magic became the only real option to get him back safely."

"Wyatt, right?"

Caleb nodded.

"Well," Jonathan said, "I appreciate not only your honesty, but the lengths to which you were willing to go to protect Caleb's pack from a black witch. I can understand your Agency's need to place you on probation, but I'm not at all worried that it will affect your ability to help us this week."

"Excuse me, sir," Matt interjected, "but I must protest. Bringing in a witch, especially one who has admitted to using blood magic, is a bad idea."

"You have already voiced your concerns, Matt, and I have taken them into consideration," Jonathan explained politely but firmly. "But at this time, I think we're better off with her than without her."

"But sir–" Matt began, but Jonathan cut him off by raising his hand.

"The discussion is over, Matt," he said calmly.

"Yes, Alpha," Matt said, lowering his eyes and closing his

mouth.

"So," Jonathan continued, turning back to Angel, "has Caleb told you about what's going on here?"

"He told me it was a conference for the North American Alphas," she answered, "and you might need some additional security, but that was all. He said the full explanation would have to come from you."

"Correct," Jonathan told her. "I wanted to wait until I was able to meet you in person to explain the situation. We've been planning this conference for several months now, and as expected when a large gathering of non-humans occurs, there have been some whispers and grumblings. Now, most of them are nothing, but there has been some talk that concerned me enough to look into it a little more. There have been whispers of the possibility that vampires might be targeting the conference."

Angel turned to Caleb, pinning him with a meaningful stare.

"I'm not sure if I should be flattered or insulted that you thought of me when you heard the word 'vampire.'" Caleb grinned, and Angel rolled her eyes, then turned back to Jonathan. "Are you sure?"

"I had a hard time believing it at first as well." Jonathan told her. "Vampires don't generally bother wolves. Partly because our blood is poisonous to them, partly because they really can't be bothered. They're too wrapped up in their own business to be concerned with other species. But I've had some of my people look into it, and there does seem to be a lot of strange vampire behavior in the last few months."

"Have you spoken to the Clan Leaders?" Angel asked.

Much like witches and wolves, vampires had their own governing body. A group of three vampires served as Clan Leaders on each continent, overseeing any and all vampire-related issues. One of their biggest jobs was to make sure their people didn't run wild and cause problems with other species.

"I have," Jonathan replied, "but they've told me they

know nothing about these threats, nor do they condone them."

"Quite the political response," Angel noted. "You'd think they'd take something like this a little more seriously."

"It's possible they know more than they are saying, but not enough to do anything about it yet," Jonathan said. "Either way, we're not getting any help from them."

Angel nodded, then glanced at Caleb. "Have you told him about Jones?"

"I told him what I know - that Jones believed the vampires were building an army, but you probably have more information than I do."

"Yeah." She paused and ran her fingers through her hair. "The black witch who threatened Caleb's pack was named Marcus Jones. He was a former WEA Agent who got a case about a missing family. It turns out they were taken by vampires, and by the time he found them, it was too late. Jones barely made it out alive. When he recovered, he started trying to convince everyone it wasn't an isolated incident. He believed the vampires were amassing an army, and they needed to stop them."

"Did they look into it?" Jonathan asked.

Angel shook her head.

"Not as far as I know. The man had witnessed something horrifying and nearly died - they assumed he had a mental break. That's when he started using blood magic, and the rest you already know."

"So what you're saying is that the witches might have known about this years ago and they did nothing about it?" Matt asked, his tone accusatory.

Angel stood and turned to face him. "The WEA may not be perfect, be they do the best they can with what they have. Are you going to try and tell me no Alpha has ever let anything slip through the cracks?"

"Enough." Jonathan spoke only a single word, but it held a lot of power. They both fell silent, and Angel sat, forcing herself to look away from Matt. "Thank you for sharing this information with us, Angel. It is entirely possible that Jones was right, but it's also entirely possible that he was just a sick man. We'll probably never know, and it makes no difference now."

Angel took a deep breath and sighed. The Master Alpha was right; they couldn't change the past, they could just do their best with the information they had now.

"Other than these 'whispers' and the strange vampire behavior, have there been any other indications an attack might be imminent?" She asked, trying to get the conversation back on track.

"Unfortunately, yes," Jonathan replied. "Over the past few months, there have been several confirmed zombie sightings in northern Ontario and Quebec. At first glance, they appeared to be small, isolated incidents, but combined with these threats, I feel like they may be part of a bigger plan."

"Zombies!?" Angel exclaimed. And when no one else seemed to respond, she turned to Caleb. "Zombies? You have got to be kidding me!" Jumping out of her chair, she started to pace, her skin crawling at the mere mention of the undead monsters.

"You don't get upset about the mention of vampires, but zombies bother you this much?" Caleb asked, surprised.

"Little witch is afraid of zombies," Matt commented rudely.

Angel whirled on him. "Do you even know what a zombie is?"

"Well, duh," Matt replied, "it's a reanimated corpse. Stumbles around, chews on people."

"Wrong," Angel told him, "very, very wrong."

"Could you explain?" Jonathan asked.

"Sure," Angel replied, "gladly. So, you know what a vampire is, right? Used to be human, now they have fangs, drink blood, can't tolerate sunlight. They're stronger and faster than wolves, and so long as they can get more blood, they can recover from nearly any injury. The only way to kill them is to destroy the heart or remove the head."

"Vampires are not stronger than wolves," Matt told her.

"Yes, they are," Jonathan replied before Angel could, turning to Matt. "One-on-one, a vampire will beat a wolf any day. The only reason wolves are able to kill vampires is because we hunt in packs." He turned back to Angel. "Continue, please."

Angel nodded. "Okay, so that's vampires. Zombies are what happens when turning a human into a vampire fails. I don't know exactly what goes wrong, but a zombie is a vampire with very basic intelligence. All they want is food; they don't eat flesh, like most people think, but they aren't smart enough to find an artery to get blood from, so they just chew at the flesh until they get to the blood. The only way to control a zombie is through their maker, and even then they only understand very simple commands. Left to their own devices, zombies will just wander off, looking for food."

"I still don't see why zombies are worse than vampires," Jesse said.

"Because," Angel explained, "if you hurt a vampire, it feels pain. If you hurt it badly enough, it will stop attacking you or run away to heal itself. You could chop a zombie's arm off, and it would keep chewing on you. They don't register pain, they have absolutely zero survival instinct, they just want to eat. In the past, groups of zombies would wipe out entire towns before anyone was able to stop them."

"So this is worse than we thought," Jonathan concluded.

"Definitely," Angel agreed.

"Will you help?" Jesse asked hopefully.

"Not a chance in hell," Angel told him.

"Are you sure?" Jonathan asked. "We're not even certain there is a legitimate threat. You'd be paid well, I can make sure of that."

"There's not enough money in the world," Angel told him, flopping down on the couch next to Caleb. "And if you're worried enough to consider throwing a witch into an enclosed space with a bunch of extremely dominant wolves, the threat is more than legitimate. I know you're not asking for my opinion, but I'm going to give it anyway - you should cancel the conference. A zombie attack here could decimate the werewolf leadership, and that wouldn't end well for a lot of people."

"You're right," Jonathan said, "I do believe that there's a significant threat, but there's no way we can cancel the conference. Most of the Alphas are already here or on their way. To cancel now would cause a lot of problems as well. I understand your decision, and I won't try to convince you to stay, but is there anything else you could tell us, anything that might help us if we do end up dealing with zombies?"

Angel ran her fingers through her hair, sighing deeply. "Let me see," she began, searching her memory for anything useful. "Werewolf blood is still poisonous to zombies, but for some reason it has a delayed effect on them. Also, from what I can remember, one of the few things zombies are afraid of is fire."

"That's better than nothing," Jesse commented.

"True," Jonathan agreed.

"Oh," Angel exclaimed, "if you kill a zombie's maker, the zombie dies as well. Not sure if that will help, because any reasonably intelligent vampire would just let his zombies do the dirty work."

Jonathan opened his mouth to speak but was interrupted when Angel's cell phone started going off.

"Sorry," she apologized.

Checking her phone, she saw "Mom" flashing on the screen. Angel stabbed the "Reject Call" button and stuffed the phone back into her pocket.

"Not a problem. Are there any potions that would be able to help?" Jonathan asked.

"Uh, you could maybe try some stunning spells. They might temporarily disable a zombie," Angel explained.

"What about a fire spell?" Jesse asked.

"Wouldn't work," Angel replied. "Store bought fire spells are designed to not burn flesh. Fire spells that will burn flesh are highly regulated, not publicly available, and you need a license to make or use them. Technically, I do have a license, but very little experience with those kinds of things." Her phone rang again. Again, it was her mother. Rolling her eyes, Angel turned to the wolves. "I'm really sorry, but if I don't answer, she's just going to keep calling."

"Go ahead," Jonathan insisted.

"Thank you," Angel said, standing and moving to the opposite side of the room. The wolves continued to discuss the vampire/zombie situation. Stabbing the "Answer" button, she held the phone to her ear. "Hi, Mom," she greeted her.

"Hello, dear, how are you?"

"Fine," Angel replied. "What's up?"

"I just wanted to give you a call, see how you were doing."

"I'm fine, Mom. Is that all?"

"Oh, no, dear, I wanted to remind you the Autumn Ball is this Friday. I know several of the young men from my Thanksgiving luncheon were interested in escorting you."

"Mom, I'm not going to the Autumn Ball, especially not with anyone from your luncheon."

"Why not?" Elizabeth managed to sound surprised, despite the fact that Angel had already made it clear she wouldn't be going. "They were perfectly nice gentlemen, and they were even willing to overlook how rude it was of you to leave early without saying goodbye."

"The only reason those 'gentlemen' were interested in me was because I shot William Warner. And I left because I didn't feel like being the entertainment anymore."

"Oh, Angel," her mother scolded her, "don't be so dramatic. They're interested in your work. You should take it as a compliment."

Angel rolled her eyes, held the phone away from herself, and shook it violently. It wasn't until she heard Caleb snort that she realized the wolves were all watching her. It took her a moment to realize her mother was still talking.

"...and that Dean, he was just so polite. You know his father invented a–"

"That's great, Mom," Angel said, trying to sound enthusiastic, "but I'm afraid I still won't be able to make it to the ball."

"Why not?" she demanded, though she didn't give Angel

a chance to answer. "I know you've been down about not being able to go back to work - goodness knows why you miss all that anyway - but you should see this as an opportunity to meet new people and get out of that little shack of yours."

"My house is not a shack!" Angel exclaimed.

"Honestly, Angel," her mother continued as if she hadn't said anything, "I'm surprised that place has indoor plumbing, but that's another problem entirely. You need to get out more. I'm going to come by first thing tomorrow morning, and we'll go shopping. You always complain about the dresses I pick for you, maybe this time we can find something you like. And then we can go to the spa and–"

"Gee, Mom," Angel exclaimed, "that really sounds like fun, but I won't be home tomorrow. Or the rest of the week, for that matter."

"Oh, why not?"

"I, uh, I got a job," Angel replied hesitantly.

"Oh, what kind of job?"

"Private security," Angel told her. "Some paranoid bigwig wants magical protection. He's paying big money, and basically all I have to do is wander around and make it look like I'm doing something useful."

"Oh," Elizabeth repeated, clearly disappointed. "Well, I suppose that's better than sitting around your house all day. You're sure you won't be home in time for the ball?"

"Yeah, I'm sure," Angel said, "the earliest I can leave is Saturday morning."

"Oh, well that's just too bad," her mother said. "I guess we'll have to wait until the Winter Ball, then."

"I guess so," Angel replied, trying to sound disappointed. "Anyway, I'm meeting with my client right now, so I've got to go. I'll talk to you later."

"Alright, dear, be safe, love you!"

"I will," Angel fibbed, "love you, too."

She hit the "End Call" button, stuffed her phone in her pocket, and sat back down on the couch. Caleb was grinning at her.

"One word, and I will use a tracking spell on you," she warned him. Caleb held up his hands, then mimed zipping his lip and throwing away the key. Turning to Jonathan, Angel shrugged. "Looks like you've got a witch on your security team," she told him. "But if zombies do show up, I get paid double."

"Sounds fair," Jonathan replied. "Welcome aboard."

"What does a tracking spell do?" Jesse asked.

"Turns you bright pink," Angel explained.

Jesse burst into a fit of giggles, and even Jonathan smiled at the idea of Caleb being turned bright pink.

CHAPTER 16

It took another hour to go through the security plans and fit Angel in with wolves who would work well with her. For most of the week, it seemed she would be paired with Jesse, which suited Angel just fine. Jesse didn't seem to have any problem with her being a witch, and he seemed like a generally nice guy. Caleb would be participating in several talks and discussions throughout the week, but he also took on some security jobs so he could work with Angel.

Aside from the fact that most attendees were werewolves, it seemed like your average conference. Breakfast in the morning, followed by a couple hours of talks, then lunch, then more talks, dinner, and some entertainment for the evening. There were several time slots during the week where Jonathan would hear requests and complaints from his Alphas, and he could either grant the request or act as an arbitrator for disputes between packs. Angel was assured all attendees would be made aware of her presence and warned to leave her alone, but she was still expecting a fair bit of resistance; wolves and witches just didn't tend to mix well.

After they'd sorted out the schedule, the wolves needed to discuss some additional details for the week, so Angel excused herself and headed down to the lobby. She wanted to get some additional equipment now that she had a better idea of what she might be dealing with.

"Excuse me," Angel asked the receptionist politely, "do you have a phone book I could borrow?"

"Of course, Miss," the young man replied, reaching behind the front desk and setting the large book in front of her. "Is there anything in particular you're looking for?"

"Yeah," Angel said, flipping to the yellow pages, "but I think I can manage on my own. Thanks!"

It took only a few minutes to find what she was looking for, and luckily she still had a few hours before the shops closed. She got the receptionist to call her a cab, and ten minutes later she was headed downtown. The hotel was at the very north end of the city, so the trip took about 20 minutes with traffic. Slipping the driver a few bills, Angel slid out of the cab and took a look around at what passed for the Magic District in Barrie. It was pretty small; only a few potion shops, a plant store, and a weapons shop. Grinning, Angel strode up to Carl's Weaponry, pulled open the door, and stepped inside. A bell tinkled overhead, and Angel took a good look around while a voice called out from the back room.

"Be with you in a moment!"

"No problem," she called back. These kinds of shops had always intrigued her, even though most of the weapons weren't necessary for her job. Swords of all shapes and sizes hung on the walls, longbows and crossbows sat on a shelf behind the counter, and glass cases holding knives and other small weapons were spread around the room. After about a minute, a middle-aged, balding man - who was built like a linebacker - emerged from the back room.

"How can I help you, Miss?" he asked.

"You're Carl?"

"The one and only."

Angel extended her hand. "I'm Angel, nice to meet you, Carl. Do you make all these yourself?"

"I do indeed," Carl replied, beaming, "all weapons are handmade and tested by yours truly. I do custom orders as well, usually within four to six weeks, but if you need something rushed, we can work something out."

"Sounds great," Angel told him, "but I'm afraid I don't have time for anything custom. I'm looking for some short swords, something I can wear underneath a jacket preferably."

"You are aware of the restrictions on those kinds of weapons?" Carl asked. "You're going to need a concealed weapons license in order for me to sell you anything."

"Of course," Angel replied, pulling out her wallet. "I've got a license right here."

Carl examined her license for a moment, then nodded approvingly. "Very good," he said, "let's see if I've got what you're looking for, Angel." He moved back behind the counter, reached underneath, and lifted several thin, narrow wooden boxes onto the counter top. "This here," he said, gesturing to the first box pulling off the lid, "is the simplest version I make. Made of basic steel, it's pretty durable, but it requires a lot of maintenance to keep the blades rust-free and sharp."

He held up one of the blades, and Angel was already impressed. The blade was about the length of her forearm, with a simple hilt and black leather grip.

"May I?" Angel asked, gesturing to the blade he held.

"Please be careful," Carl warned, handing her the sword hilt-first, "the blade is already sharpened."

"I will," Angel replied, taking the hilt carefully and trying to get a feel for the weight of the sword. Stepping back, she held the blade vertically and moved through a few of the exercises she'd learned in her martial arts classes. The blade was well-balanced, and comfortable to hold. "It's good," she told Carl, who smiled at the praise. She returned to the counter and set the sword gently back in its case. "What else have you got?"

"I also have blades in stainless steel, and carbon steel," he explained, opening two other cases. "Stainless steel is much more resistant to corrosion, but it's tricky to keep it sharp. Carbon steel is extremely tough and durable, and it holds an edge very well."

"Let's take a look at the carbon steel," Angel suggested.

"Very good," Carl replied, setting several cases to the side and opening three more. "This is all I have in stock currently. I have scabbards for all three, and several types of holsters that should work well for you."

Angel examined her options. The first set of swords was

single-edged, with a slight curve at the end of each blade and rather ornate handle. Not great for hiding under clothing. The second set was double-edged, with a simpler handle that would be quite easy to conceal. Definitely a contender. The third set was, in a word, amazing. Single-edged, with a significant upward curve at the end of the blades, they strongly resembled a scimitar. They flowed from hilt to blade so smoothly, Angel imagined they'd feel like natural extensions to her arms.

"Wow," she said, unable to hide how impressed she was with the quality of the swords. "These are incredible."

"Give them a try," Carl encouraged, holding the third set out to her.

Angel grasped the hilts firmly and lifted the swords from their case. They felt almost weightless, they were so perfectly balanced. Twirling them in her hands, they moved smoothly through the air.

"I think we have a winner, Carl," Angel told him, grinning widely.

Carl agreed with her choice wholeheartedly and spent the better part of the next hour helping her pick out a holster that would work well for her size, as well as putting together a little kit that would help her keep the blades well-maintained and ready to use. She also picked up a set of small knives she could hide on various parts of her body and a pair of forearm guards she hoped would stop sharp teeth. Angel handed her credit card over quite happily, glad for once her probation with work was paid.

After thanking Carl profusely and wishing him a good night, Angel went in search of something for dinner. It was shortly past 5pm, so there was no shortage of places to choose from. A pizza place that smelled divine drew her in, and after finding a booth where she could keep her recent purchases safe, she ordered an extra large meat lovers. It was delicious, and she only just managed not to laugh at the look on the waiter's face when he realized she'd eaten the whole thing.

It was dark by the time she left the restaurant, so she

hailed a cab and headed back to the hotel, planning on getting a good night's sleep before she had to deal with biased, egotistical male wolves, and possibly zombies. In the lobby, she noticed a number of wolves checking in, but they didn't give her any trouble. Angel took the stairs up to the second floor, fishing the key-card from her purse as she approached #203. For a moment before she slid the card into the reader, Angel could have sworn she heard the TV on inside her room. Assuming it was just a result of her enhanced hearing and poor soundproofing, she slid her card, the door unlocked with a click, and she slipped inside the room.

It took Angel a good minute to process what she was seeing. It was a pretty standard hotel room; bathroom to the left with towels and toiletries, two double beds, desk, TV, coffee pot, and so on. The thing that threw her, though, was Caleb, lounging shirtless on the nearest bed, eating pizza and watching a reality TV show.

"There you are," Caleb greeted her warmly. "Want some pizza?"

"Uh, I, I already ate," Angel replied, caught off guard by the question. Setting her purchases in the closet on her right, she tried to gather her thoughts. After a few moments, she managed to pull herself together and ask the burning question. "What are you doing here?"

"Eating dinner," Caleb answered, "and watching TV."

"Yeah, I figured that out," Angel said. "But why are you doing it in my room?"

"Our room," Caleb corrected, watching the television intently.

"What do you mean, 'our room?'" Angel demanded.

"There weren't any more rooms available, so I figured we could just share instead of you staying at another hotel across town," he explained, finally looking away from the television. "You're okay with that, right?"

Angel opened her mouth to say "No," but the word got stuck in her throat. Caleb looked at her, an innocent smile plastered on his face, and she knew he hadn't just forgotten to tell her about the sleeping arrangements. It frustrated and excited her more than she thought possible. He'd set a trap, and she'd walked right into it. Her wolf was impressed, and if she was being honest, so was she.

"Yeah, sure," she lied, "works for me." Caleb grinned and went back to watching his show, but upon closer inspection, Angel could see he was watching her closely. Spotting her bags on the farthest bed, she strode across the room and grabbed the duffel with her clothes. "I'm gonna take a shower," she told him, stepping into the bathroom and closing the door before he had a chance to respond.

Angel locked the door, dumped her bag on the tile floor, and turned the shower on full blast. Leaning against the counter top, she stared into the mirror, hoping the person looking back might be able to help her figure out what to do. Her wolf was surprisingly quiet, and Angel wasn't sure how to feel about that. Either her other half had finally decided to let her make the decisions when it came to Caleb, or the wolf knew the decision was already made.

Stripping quickly, Angel stepped into the shower, reveling in the feel of the hot water on her skin. She knew what she wanted, knew what her wolf wanted, but up until this point, fear had held her back. Caleb didn't know they were Mates, but clearly something attracted him to Angel. Maybe he, or his wolf, sensed it without realizing what it was. If that was the case, what did it mean for the future? Would he eventually come to the conclusion that she was his Mate, or would she need to tell him the truth to keep from losing him? If it were the latter, could they handle the consequences?

Stamping her foot, Angel cursed under her breath and dispensed a large amount of hotel shampoo into her palm. Washing her hair helped calm her down, the light floral scent quickly spreading throughout the room. The body wash smelled like mint and tingled on her skin; Angel took her time in the shower, knowing she'd have to make a decision before she left the bathroom. The room was filled with steam, and the mirror was completely fogged up by the time Angel turned off the water and grabbed a towel. She dried herself off, wrapped the towel around her torso, stepped out of the tub, and wiped a section of the mirror clear. Her reflection stared back at her, almost daring her to take a chance.

"Fuck it," she whispered under her breath.

Reaching for her duffel bag, she started searching for clean clothes, pausing after a moment. A sly grin spread across her face. Dropping the towel on the floor, she reached for the door, took a deep breath, and turned the handle. For a moment, her courage failed her, and Angel found herself standing just inside the bathroom.

"Look, Angel," Caleb's voice came from the other room, "I'm sorry about the room situation. I should have told you ahead of time. I'm sorry. If you want, I'll see if I can find somewhere else to stay."

He was giving her an out, and it was an easy one. All she had to do was close the door, and he would never know. Her wolf growled inside her head, and Angel got the message: they didn't take the easy way, it wasn't nearly as much fun. Taking another deep breath, she stepped into the room.

CHAPTER 17

When Angel had escaped into the bathroom, Caleb started doubting his plan for the first time since he'd thought it up. Aside from the obvious surprise at finding out they'd be sharing a room, she'd been completely unreadable. He'd honestly been hoping she'd get mad, since that had worked out so well for him the night Cassie was born. Instead, she just grabbed her bag and locked herself in the bathroom. For over thirty minutes. What if she was freaking out? What if she was putting together a nasty spell to knock him out and escape? What if she was calling Sara? His mind raced with all the possible answers, each one worse than the last. By the time the shower turned off, he was fully prepared to apologize and sleep in the hallway. The bathroom door opened, but Angel didn't come out.

"Look, Angel," he said, hoping his sincerity came through in his voice. "I'm sorry about the room situation. I should have told you ahead of time. I'm sorry. If you want, I'll see if I can find somewhere else to stay."

She didn't answer, but a moment later she stepped into the room. Completely naked. Caleb actually had to pinch himself to make sure he wasn't dreaming.

"Uh, I, uh," he stammered, unable to form a complete sentence.

He'd always thought Angel was beautiful, and he'd already seen her naked, but the circumstances had been completely different. Now here she was, standing proud, tall, and naked before him, and he'd never seen anything more wonderful. Standing, he approached her slowly, afraid he might make a wrong move and scare her away. She laughed, and it was a beautiful sound.

"I'm not going anywhere," she told him.

He stood before her now and extended his arms, trailing his fingertips across her hips and around to her back. Pulling her against him, he stared down into her eyes. Angel smiled up at him, then wrapped her arms around his neck and pulled him down for a scorching kiss. His body came alive instantly, and Caleb could tell she was feeling the same way. Her scent surrounded him, strong and sweet, and it took every bit of his self-control not to throw her on the bed and take her now. But he had to be careful; she was a witch, and as tough as she seemed, he could still hurt her if he wasn't careful. Reaching his hands lower, Caleb cupped her buttocks in his palms, lifting her off the ground. Angel wrapped her legs around his waist, pressing her center against his very hard cock and making him moan out loud. Angel leaned back, breaking the kiss, and watched him thoughtfully for a moment before slowly rocking her hips against him.

"Stop," he managed to growl out.

"Why?" she asked, slowing her movements instead.

"I don't want to hurt you."

She grinned at him and said, "I'm not nearly as fragile as you think."

"You are, and I don't want to mess this up."

Angel watched him for a moment, holding still while she contemplated him. Then, leaning towards him again, she brushed her lips along his jaw, then his throat, and finally up to his ear.

"You won't," she told him, "I trust you, and I know you well enough that you'd never hurt me, even accidentally. But," she lowered her voice to barely a whisper, her breath tickling him softly, "if you aren't fucking me in the next five minutes, I'll take you up on your offer to find somewhere else to sleep."

Angel wasn't sure if it was telling him she trusted him or the imposed deadline, but she'd never seen someone change their tune so quickly. One moment they were standing - Angel's legs wrapped around his waist, and Caleb's hands holding her ass - and the next she was flat on her back on the bed. He joined her a minute later, having removed his pants. Angel adored the feel of his bare skin against hers, running her hands over his arms, his back, and anywhere else she could reach. He kissed her deeply, leaving her breathless, then kissed and nibbled his way down her throat, to her collarbone. She could feel his erection - long and hard - pressing against her thigh, and it was all she could do not to scream at him to hurry up. His hands found her breasts, kneading them gently; he pinched her nipples, and she arched her back at the spike of desire that rushed through her. His mouth moved lower, and he planted soft kisses on her breasts before pulling one nipple into his mouth and sucking gently. She moaned out loud at the feeling, and he sucked harder.

"Fuck!" Angel shouted, fisting her hands in his hair. He switched to the other one and received the same reaction. When he moved to go lower, Angel pulled him back up. "Now," she panted, "please!"

Caleb grinned, trailing a hand down her stomach, stroking softly between her legs. Her body tensed, and her breath came in shallow gasps.

"Please," she repeated.

He continued to tease her, stroking her softly, grazing her clit with each movement and watching her reaction. Angel felt like she was going to combust, the sensations were so intense, and all she could think of was how wonderful it would be to go out like this. Just when she thought she wouldn't be able to handle any more, Caleb slid a finger inside her, and Angel came so hard, she swore she saw stars.

When she came back to herself, Caleb was kneeling between her legs and watching her intently. He smiled at her, and she smiled back, nodding slowly. Ever so gently, he slid forward, pressing his cock inside her, inch by wonderful inch. Angel wrapped her legs around his waist, urging him deeper. When he was fully inside her, he paused a moment, letting her adjust to his size. He was large - as most werewolves were - and though he filled her completely, it wasn't at all uncomfortable. He slid back slowly, until he almost left her completely, then pushed forward again, just as slowly. The pace was far too slow for Angel's liking - she tried rocking her hips to increase the pace, but he grabbed her waist and held her still. She tried digging her heels into his buttocks, but he ignored her efforts and continued with his slow, steady thrusts.

"Faster," she demanded, but he only chuckled in response. It was maddening; having him inside her felt so amazing, but she needed hard and fast, not slow and gentle. "Please," she begged him, "harder." He thrust once - hard and fast - and she gasped at the sensation. "Yes," she urged. He did it again, and she arched her back. He leaned forward, planting his hands on either side of her head and brushing his lips against hers.

"Tell me what you want," Caleb whispered.

"I want you," she answered, pressing her hips against his encouragingly.

"You're sure?"

"Yes!"

He growled loudly before pressing his lips against hers roughly, thrusting into her hard and fast. She moaned out loud, not caring that the flimsy hotel walls would likely carry her cries down the hallway. Her whole body shook with the force of his thrusts, and she wrapped her arms around his shoulders, buried her face in the crook of his neck, and held on tight. For the second time that night, she felt herself coming apart at the seams, but this time she was ready. Her orgasm came almost too quickly, slamming into her and moving like a wave through her whole body. Caleb came a moment later, shouting out and thrusting deep inside her one last time.

They lay together for a few minutes, panting heavily and trying to catch their breath. Eventually, Caleb slid out of her, lying on his side and pulling Angel close. For a few minutes, Angel thought he was going to say something, or maybe that she should say something, but thankfully this was one of those comfortable silences. Snuggling into his shoulder, she inhaled his scent, feeling calmer and more relaxed than she had in months. In a matter of minutes, she drifted off to sleep.

Sex with Angel had been all Caleb had expected, and then some. She was aggressive, demanding, and so damn responsive to his touch. He had to admit, she'd been more than worth the wait. She fell asleep in his arms that night, and he was surprised at how right it felt. His wolf agreed, but it still left a lot of questions unanswered, including why she'd avoided him for so long, and if she could actually be his Mate. He had a feeling figuring out the answer to the first question would help him answer the second one, but he had no idea how to get her to tell him.

Watching her sleep, Caleb realized she'd taken a big step tonight, and if he was patient, she'd eventually trust him enough to tell him the truth. Pulling the blankets over them both, he pulled her closer, closed his eyes, and drifted off to sleep.

CHAPTER 18

Jonathan sat at the too-small desk in his hotel room. It was late, and he knew the right thing to do was get to bed and get some sleep, but his mind refused to quiet down. Not wanting to bother with the coffee machine in the hotel lobby, he grabbed a cup of cold coffee from the brewer in the kitchenette and popped it into the microwave to reheat. Coffee in hand, he grabbed the folder containing all the information on the vampire threats and sat down on the couch. He'd read everything already, but he re-examined each document, making sure he hadn't missed anything important.

War with the vampires - even a small group - was certainly not something he wanted. While wolves typically won in small skirmishes between the two species, vampires were inherently stronger. It was also more difficult to tell just how many vampires there were in any given area. The Clan Leaders would likely have a good idea, but they weren't sharing that information with anyone. So for all he knew, the vampires could outnumber the wolves, and that would be bad. Throw in some zombies, and they were in real trouble.

When nothing new jumped out at him, Jonathan replaced everything in the folder and set it aside. He paced the room, going over the schedule for the next day in his head. Eventually, his thoughts strayed to the witch Caleb had brought to help. He'd met many witches over his lifetime, and Angel was unlike most. She knew about wolves, enough to navigate social situations that usually left most people confused or even upset. She was strong-willed, and from what he'd heard from Caleb, a very powerful witch. Jesse had taken to her well, and Matt had at least remained mostly quiet with his objections. He was hoping there wouldn't be any issues with having her around this week, but even still, he felt better knowing they had something of an ace up their sleeve if any uninvited guests did arrive. Eventually, there was nothing more that needed to be done, and Jonathan found himself puttering. Knowing he needed as much rest as possible for the coming days, he headed for bed.

CHAPTER 19

Alice huddled in the corner with the others, not because she was cold, but because it was better than being alone. She didn't feel the cold anymore. She didn't feel much of anything except hunger. The ones who kept them there brought them food every day, and despite how much her mind rebelled at the idea, she ate what they provided. But there wasn't nearly enough for everyone to have their fill. The hunger always remained, just below the surface. It was like a living, breathing creature, just waiting to burst forth and consume everything in its path. Just yesterday, a fight had broken out among several of the new arrivals, each of them trying to get their hands on more than their fair share. Their keepers had not been pleased. They'd pulled apart the brawlers and dragged them away, kicking and screaming.

"No fighting," ordered the tall, dark-haired male wearing a bloodstained blue polo.

No one had seen those newcomers since. She shivered in fear, not knowing if where they'd gone was better or worse than here.

CHAPTER 20

The alarm on Angel's phone went off at 5am. Climbing out of bed, she rummaged through her purse to find the device, turning off the alarm. Tossing the phone on the dresser, she stood and stretched, rubbing the sleep from her eyes.

"I was going to complain about the rude awakening," Caleb commented from the bed, "but I can't say I mind the view."

Angel turned quickly, realizing she was standing naked in the middle of the room and Caleb was watching her closely. She had a moment of panic and self-consciousness, both of which were quickly derailed when she noticed how damn sexy he looked in the morning. His hair was rumpled, his voice was a little gravelly, and Angel couldn't help thinking of all the wonderful parts currently hidden by the blankets.

"Sorry," she apologized, finding it very difficult to keep her eyes off his naked upper body.

Caleb stretched slowly - maybe a little too slowly - then sat up, leaning back against the headboard.

"Why are you up so early anyway?"

"I, uh, usually go for a run in the morning," Angel replied, tearing her eyes away from him and looking around for her bag of clothes. She'd just remembered it was in the bathroom when Caleb grabbed her around the waist and pulled her back onto the bed.

"I'll give you a workout," he told her, pressing kisses along her shoulder and up her neck.

He nipped at her earlobe, and she gasped as her whole body came alive. Turning in his arms, Angel straddled him, leaning forward so her breasts pressed against his chest and her center pressed against his erection.

"Will you, now?" she asked, and he growled, low and deep, before flipping her onto her back. He parted her legs with his knee while he leaned forward to kiss her deeply. Angel had to admit, this was way better than a morning run.

After a quick romp in bed, Angel headed to the bathroom for a shower, grinning from ear to ear. She'd just started to wash her hair when Caleb joined her, picking her up, pressing her back against the shower wall, and slipping inside her. After leaving her breathless and a little weak in the knees, he washed quickly, gave her a quick peck on the cheek, and left her to finish on her own. She stepped out of the bathroom a few minutes later, drying her hair with a towel, to see him already dressed.

"Where are you off to?"

"I've got a quick meeting this morning with a couple packs," he explained, "all sorts of fun political crap. I'll meet you at Jonathan's room at eight for the security debrief."

"Okay," she replied, a little sad they wouldn't get more time alone this morning.

He must have noticed something in her voice, because Caleb wrapped his arms around her and kissed her deeply.

"Don't worry," he told her, "we'll get lots of time together later."

Angel grinned and blushed, surprised at how easily he read her mood.

"Okay," she told him, and this time she meant it.

"Good," he nodded, gave her another quick kiss, and left the room.

Deciding she didn't want to give herself too much time to overanalyze the recent developments between her and Caleb, Angel decided she would head downstairs for breakfast. She dressed quickly, then pulled out her purchases from last night. The harness she'd picked for the short swords was perfect. She put her arms through the holes, and leather straps crisscrossed her back; the sheaths for each sword attached to the harness with simple but strong clips. The sheaths were attached upside-down, so the handles for each sword rested just at her waist, and well within reach. Magnets kept the blades from falling out. She pulled on the forearm guards, then her jacket, pleasantly surprised at how well the blades were concealed. Pulling out the small throwing knives she'd also picked up, she tucked two into her boots, two onto her belt, and two up her sleeves; those ones were held in place by a small spell. She grabbed a couple stunning spells, and a few healing spells, just in case, before deciding she was as ready as she'd ever be.

Leaving her room, she headed toward the stairs - she had no intention of getting herself trapped in the elevator with any strange wolves - following the smell of food to the restaurant inside the hotel. It was early, only 7:30, but the place was still pretty busy. Most of the tables were occupied by wolves, and more than one watched her as she approached the breakfast buffet. Trying to ignore their stares, Angel grabbed a plate and filled it with eggs, bacon, and several large pancakes. She poured herself a large cup of coffee and found an unoccupied table to sit at while she ate.

Surprisingly, Angel made it through her entire breakfast - two plates of the buffet and a couple muffins on the side - without any real issue. A lot of the wolves kept staring at her, and she heard several whispered conversations, but no one addressed her directly. Leaving the restaurant, she again took the stairs, stepping out on the fourth floor. As she approached the Master Alpha's room, she saw Jesse standing outside. He smiled at her, and she found herself smiling back.

"Morning," he greeted.

"Morning."

"I see you managed to make it through breakfast alright," he commented, "the way Caleb talked, I figured we'd have some kind of brawl before this thing even started."

"I'm not that bad," Angel complained.

"Don't worry about it," Jesse told her, clapping her on the shoulder. "Around here, it's better to have a reputation. It makes people think twice before they mess with you."

He opened his mouth like he was going to say something else, but a strange look crossed his face. Before Angel realized what he was doing, he leaned down and inhaled deeply, scenting her. A moment later, he pulled back, grinning at her.

"What?" she asked, a little confused.

"You smell like Caleb," he told her.

Angel flushed crimson. "Oh, hell," she cursed. Of course she smelled like Caleb, and of course Jesse - and any other wolf, for that matter - would be able to figure out why.

"Relax," Jesse told her, "it's probably not a bad thing. People will be less likely to mess with you, since they probably don't want to mess with Caleb."

"Yeah, but they'll think the only reason I'm here is because Caleb and I are..."

"Having sex?" Jesse finished for her, laughing when she blushed again.

"You're not helping," she told him.

"No, but it's not like there's anything you can do about it," Jesse said.

"I could whip up a spell to hide it," Angel suggested.

"Oh, no," Jesse held his hands up in warning. "That's a bad idea. Male wolves don't leave their scent on a female for no reason," he explained. "They do it to warn off other males. If you hide his scent, Caleb might get upset."

"So, basically, I might as well have 'Property of Caleb' stamped on my forehead," Angel summarized, "and there's nothing I can do about it?"

"Yep."

"Great," Angel sighed, "just great."

"Don't worry about it," Jesse assured her, "it'll be fine. Now come on, we're almost ready to get started."

He pulled out a key card and opened the door, holding it open so Angel could enter first. She stepped into the room, and every eye turned to look at her. A lot more wolves were in there today - at least a dozen, if not more - and Angel tried really hard not to let her nerves show. Matt was there again, and he still looked unhappy to see her, which wasn't really a surprise. Most of the rest of the wolves just seemed curious, though, which Angel hoped was a good sign. She scanned the room for Caleb but didn't see him. She was planning on just hanging out in the back, but Jesse motioned for her to stand next to him, near the front. After a few minutes, Caleb arrived. He joined her near the front, standing on her other side.

"Look at that," he said quietly, so only she and Jesse could hear, "on your own for nearly an hour, and nothing's on fire yet."

"Ass," Angel whispered back, punching him in the arm.

Jesse laughed. Caleb looked like he was going to say something else, but Jonathan entered the room, immediately drawing everyone's attention.

"Hello, everyone," Jonathan greeted. "I trust everyone has received their assignments for the week?" Several people answered, "Yes," but most just nodded. "Excellent," he continued. "There are a few updates I wanted to pass along personally. Firstly, as some of you may have noticed, we have a witch joining us today." Jonathan gestured to Angel, who smiled politely and gave a little wave. "Miss Myers is here to lend her expertise and help make sure we have a safe, productive conference. She is here at my request, and as such, I expect you all to treat her accordingly."

He paused, letting his words sink in, and Angel was starting to understand why he was the Master Alpha. His power was subtle; he didn't often give direct orders, but he still gave orders she suspected his wolves would have a hard time disobeying.

"Why, exactly, do we need a witch to help us with security?" The question came from a beefy wolf near the front.

"That is an excellent question," Jonathan said, "and leads very well into my second update. There have been threats made against this conference by vampires. There is also a chance that we may encounter zombies as well. Having a witch working with us may limit the damage that either of these threats pose. If you have any additional questions, please speak with Jesse, Matt, or Caleb. Now, are there any more questions?" No one spoke up, and Jonathan nodded approvingly. "Very good. Now if everyone could please see to their assignments, the conference will be starting shortly."

The room cleared out quickly, with only a few wolves hanging behind to give Angel a few curious looks. After a few minutes, only Angel, Jesse, Caleb, Matt, and Jonathan remained.

"Well," Jesse said brightly, clapping Angel on the shoulder, "I think that went well." Caleb gave the other male a pointed look, and Jessie dropped his hand. "Relax, Caleb," he said, "I'm not interested in your witch. I've got a Mate, remember?"

"Right," Caleb said, "I know."

"Ugh," Angel groaned, "please cut it out with the alpha male bullshit."

"That's what you get for getting involved with an alpha male," Jesse told her, flopping down on the couch.

Angel crossed her arms and made a face at him.

"Children," Jonathan scolded playfully. "Is this going to be a problem?"

He motioned at Angel and Caleb.

"No," Angel replied quickly.

"Nope," Caleb replied.

Jonathan considered them for a moment before nodding.

"Alright," he said. "Angel, I believe you and Jesse are assigned to the perimeter today. You were going to set up some wards to detect any unwanted visitors, I believe?"

"That's right," Angel told him, "should be pretty straightforward."

"Good, keep me updated," Jonathan said, "I'll be in talks most of the day, but I've got a break at lunchtime and right before supper."

"And I'll switch out with Jesse for a few hours this afternoon," Caleb added.

"Anyone have any questions before we get things started?" Jonathan asked.

"Yeah," Matt replied, gesturing to Angel. "Shouldn't you

have some sort of weapon or something?"

"I'm a witch," Angel replied, "I am a weapon. But if that's not convincing enough for you, I did pick up a few things last night."

Stepping away from the wall, she reached behind her back and pulled her new swords free from their sheaths. They slid free quickly and quietly.

Jesse whistled appreciatively.

"Nice hardware."

Matt scoffed. "Do you even know how to use those?" he asked condescendingly.

"Nope," Angel replied, sick of his attitude, "I just thought I would flail them around a bunch and see what happens."

Jesse and Caleb laughed, and she could have sworn Jonathan chuckled a little. Matt just gave her a nasty look.

"I'm going to do a final sweep of the conference rooms," he said, turning and leaving the room.

"Well," Angel said, pretending to check a watch, "less than twenty-four hours, and I'm already making friends."

"Don't mind Matt," Jonathan told her, "he takes a while to warm up to people."

"If you say so," she replied, convinced it was either her gender or species Matt had a problem with, not the fact that she was a new face. Sliding the blades back into their sheaths, she turned to Jesse. "Should we get going?"

"Sure," Jesse said, hopping up from the couch, "let's go."

Angel followed him, turning to Caleb when she reached the door and giving him a little wave.

"See you later," she said.

"Don't start any fights you can't finish," Caleb said, winking at her.

"You say that like it should be easy," Angel joked, stepping into the hallway.

CHAPTER 21

They headed for the stairs, at Angel's request, then Jesse led them out of the hotel and along the path they'd chosen to be their perimeter. Thankfully, there weren't a lot of other buildings around the hotel. This area of the city was pretty sparse, with a forest to the north of the hotel, the highway to the south, and some warehouses a couple blocks down on either side. Jesse and Matt had already checked out the warehouses, and the forest to the north, and found nothing out of the ordinary. Still, it was possible they'd missed something, so Angel was going to set up a magical ward around the hotel that would go off if something without a heartbeat got too close.

They started to the north, just at the tree line. Wards weren't particularly difficult to put in place; all you needed was a bit of magic and a good idea of how you wanted it to work. The simpler the ward, the easier it was to set up and maintain. If you tried to make it do too much, it might not work correctly, or it might stop working too soon. Angel pulled a bag of marbles from her belt and poured the small round stones into her hand.

"What are those for?" Jesse asked.

"Focusing objects," Angel explained, "they'll make the ward stronger and easier to set up. I cast the spell over all of them, then set up an anchor point, and all I have to do after that is drop marbles along the perimeter. Then when we loop back around to the anchor point, I fuse the ends, and we've got a ward."

"What if someone moves the marbles?"

"Once the ward is set up, the marbles won't be visible," Angel told him, "but if someone is able to see through the magic that hides them, and moves them, I'll know."

"So you'll be the only one who knows if the ward is breached?"

"That's generally how wards work, but I can use a couple of the leftover marbles to make beacons. That way, whoever has the beacons will also know when the ward is breached."

"Cool," Jesse exclaimed. "Is there anything I can do to help?"

"Just stand back, and try not to interrupt me," Angel said. "I need to concentrate for a couple minutes."

Angel stared at the marbles, quieting her thoughts and focusing on exactly what she needed the ward to do. After a few minutes, she was ready. Taking a deep breath, she wove the magic for a ward around the small stones, imbuing the magic with her intent. The magic surrounded the marbles instead of soaking into them; ward magic didn't need to be that durable, and this way she would be able to re-use the marbles in the future. After a few minutes, the magic was in place, and the ward was ready to be set up. Angel picked out a single marble, placing it just in front of her and pushing a small amount of magic into it - activating the ward. It glowed brightly for a moment, then the light faded to a soft glow, just enough to see it in the long grass.

"That's it?" Jesse asked, watching the marble curiously.

"Pretty much," Angel replied. "Now we just need to place the rest of these every fifty feet or so." She headed west, counting her steps to estimate how far she was from the anchor.

"Would someone else be able to feel it when they pass through?" Jesse asked.

"Depends," Angel replied, reaching fifty and placing a marble on the ground. "A witch will definitely sense it, they might even be able to figure out what it's for, too. Most wolves are sensitive enough that they'll probably feel it, but they might not realize what it is." She placed a third marble on the ground. They were approaching the hotel parking lot now. "A vampire would probably also feel it, if they're old enough."

"What about zombies?"

"They might feel it," Angel replied, "but they wouldn't

have the mental capacity to really know what it was."

They were at the front of the hotel now, about halfway around the perimeter. Angel placed another marble on the ground, and they kept walking.

"So," Jesse began, "Caleb tells me you're pretty badass."

"Does he, now?" Angel replied, curious to know what Caleb had told Jesse, or for that matter, Jonathan.

"Yeah," Jesse said, "the way he tells it, you saved his whole damn pack."

"I was just doing my job."

Jesse scoffed.

"Yeah, right," he said, "there aren't a lot of witches who would risk their lives to save a bunch of wolves."

"I wish I could disagree with you," Angel said, "but unfortunately, that sentiment seems to work both ways."

"True," Jesse admitted, "but there seems to be some decent people on either side. Almost makes up for all the idiots."

"Almost," Angel agreed.

They fell into silence for a little while, but Angel could tell Jesse still had things he wanted to ask. He managed to keep it to himself for a whole two minutes.

"Is it true you killed one of Caleb's wolves?"

"Yes," Angel admitted, "but don't mention it in front of Caleb."

"Why?"

"Because it upsets him," Angel explained. "Roscoe almost killed me, after Caleb made it clear I was his guest. He blames himself."

"Got it," Jesse said. He paused a moment, then spoke again. "So, what's the deal with you two? You dating?"

"I, uh, don't really know," Angel admitted, "we haven't really discussed anything like that yet."

"You do realize he's head over heels for you, right?"

"Don't be ridiculous," Angel told Jesse, not allowing herself to believe such a crazy idea.

"Seriously?" Jesse stepped in front of her, forcing her to

stop. "I - a Mated male and one of Caleb's good friends - put my hand on your shoulder, and he gave me the 'get your hand off her if you want to keep it attached to your arm' look. He's got it bad."

"Really?" Angel asked, still not completely convinced.

"Really," Jesse insisted. "So if you don't feel the same way, you should probably let him know. It might be easier on both of you."

"I, uh, don't really know how I feel yet," Angel fibbed.

She knew exactly how she felt - she loved Caleb more than she would ever love another man - but she was still afraid of what would happen if he found out her secret.

"Best work on that," Jesse suggested, stepping out of her way.

They fell silent for a few moments, and Angel couldn't help starting to overthink her situation with Caleb. It wasn't anything new, and it threatened to give her a headache. Wanting to distract herself, and grateful for a mostly independent third party, she decided to ask Jesse a few questions she'd collected about packs.

"What's the difference between pack bonds and Mate bonds? I've read books about werewolves, and none of them goes into any real detail, but they definitely seem important."

Jesse nodded. "They are important, which is part of the reason why we don't really make the exact details publicly available."

"Someone could use them against you?"

"Exactly. But I don't think you would."

Angel shook her head. "Of course not."

"Good. Well, let's start with pack bonds. They're hierarchical in nature - starting from the bottom with the most submissive member of the pack, and going all the way up to the Alpha. Pack bonds can be formed in one of two ways. The first way is when the Alpha or their Mate claims an individual as part of their pack with a bite. The second way is when an existing pack member claims a Mate, which includes them in the pack bonds automatically."

"What happens when the mate already belongs to a pack?"

"Traditionally, the mated pair will belong to the male's pack, but there's plenty of times where they choose to belong to the female's pack instead. That does require a little cooperation from both Alphas, but it's usually just a formality."

"OK, that's pretty straightforward. What about Mate bonds?"

"Mate bonds are a little different. Obviously, anyone can form a Mate bond, but it does require acceptance from both parties. Mate bonds are also balanced - neither partner has more power than the other."

"That's how an Alpha's Mate is able to create pack bonds, then, right?"

"Exactly."

"Huh. That's neat. I mean, werewolves have always seemed so decidedly patriarchal to me, I guess I expected Mate bonds to still favor the male."

"You're not wrong. Up until a few decades ago, the only way a female could be recognized as dominant was through her mate. But most packs, especially the ones in North America, are getting better at recognizing their female pack mates who are dominant on their own."

"That's great. Thanks for explaining all that to me. And, uh, thanks for your advice about Caleb."

Jesse nodded and gave her a small smile. "No problem."

They finished setting up the ward, did one last perimeter sweep, then headed back inside. It was mid-morning, and Caleb and Jonathan were still in one of the conference rooms, so they tracked down Matt, giving him one of the marble beacons. He scowled at the little stone but stuck it in his pocket anyway, then headed off to check something vague. Angel figured he just didn't want to be around her, which she was okay with; she didn't really like being around him either.

Jesse led her on a tour around the hotel, showing her

the various conference rooms and dining halls they would be using throughout the week. They ended the tour at the main dining hall, just as the hotel staff were starting to set up the lunch buffet. Everything smelled delicious, and she and Jesse were able to snag a couple plates of food early, since they were going to be Jonathan's personal security for lunch and the first half of the afternoon. Lunchtime came, and the dining hall filled quickly with wolves who had been attending the morning talks. Jonathan grabbed a plate, then sat at the head table, with Angel and Jesse at his back. They updated him quickly on the ward and gave him the beacon.

"If anything triggers the ward," Angel explained, "the beacon will glow brightly and beep until you pick it up."

"Excellent," Jonathan told her, "thank you very much."

They spent the rest of lunch standing behind him, watching the room for anything out of the ordinary. Thankfully, no vampires jumped out from under the tables, which made sense since it was the middle of the day. After everyone had eaten, they moved into one of the smaller conference rooms. Angel nearly fell asleep, having to stand still and listen to people ramble on and on. When three o'clock rolled around, she was immensely grateful for a break. Caleb was waiting for her outside of the conference room, and she couldn't help smiling when she saw him.

"Hey," he greeted her. "How's it going?"

"Peachy," Angel replied, coming to stand before him. "I set up the ward this morning, and we haven't had any troubles. How about you?"

"Not bad," he told her. He pulled her out of the way of a bunch of wolves who didn't seem inclined to alter their path enough to avoid her. He cast them a nasty look. "We've got about twenty minutes before Jonathan needs us. Wanna go grab a snack?"

"Sure," she said, allowing him to take her hand and lead her through the crowd.

It felt strange to be holding his hand, but in a good way.

She barely even noticed the weird looks they were getting from some of the wolves they passed. Caleb led her to the hotel restaurant, where only a few others were grabbing a mid-afternoon meal. They had a near-constant buffet set up for the conference, so Caleb just grabbed a plate, loaded it up with sandwiches, and sat down at one of the tables in the back. Angel grabbed them some drinks and joined him.

"So what's the Autumn Ball?" Caleb asked after inhaling his first sandwich.

"Ugh," Angel groaned.

Caleb laughed at her. "It can't be that bad," he insisted.

"It's a ball," Angel said, stressing the word "ball." "Fancy clothes, tiny little hors d'oeuvres, and no hard liquor - it's awful. My mother seems to think I'm gonna be like friggin' Cinderella, find Prince Charming, and live happily ever after in high society."

"I'm having a hard time picturing you in a fancy dress," Caleb admitted, looking her up and down.

"It's painful, trust me," Angel told him, "especially the frilly things my mother always picks out for me."

"What happened at your mom's Thanksgiving luncheon?"

Angel groaned again. "You know, you could at least pretend you weren't eavesdropping," she told him.

"Sorry," Caleb apologized, "wolf hearing - it's kinda hard not to."

"Right," Angel nodded, and when it didn't seem like she was going to answer the question, Caleb gave her a go on gesture. "OK, fine, the luncheon. My mother was trying to play matchmaker again, so she sat me at a table with a bunch of single guys. Ignoring the fact that none of them were even remotely my type; all they were interested in was what happened with William. One of them even invited me to the ball, just because he wanted to see how William would react when he saw me."

"That sucks," Caleb summarized, and she agreed wholeheartedly. "It seems like your mom just wants you to be happy, though. It's nice, in an overbearing kind of way."

"She wants me to be happy, so long as it fits into her idea of how things should be," Angel corrected him. "Don't get me wrong, I love my mom, but she needs to realize I'm not anything like her, and what she thinks will make me happy and what actually makes me happy are two very different things."

"I'm sure she'll figure it out eventually," Caleb assured her, reaching across the table and taking her hand in his. He smiled and gave her hand a little squeeze.

"Thanks," Angel replied, smiling back.

The rest of the afternoon passed without incident; Angel and Caleb were assigned to guard Jonathan, which basically meant standing behind him while he or another wolf talked a lot. By the time they were done for the day, Angel was itching to go for a run. They entered their hotel room, and Angel started digging through her duffel bag.

"What are you looking for?" Caleb asked

"Running clothes," Angel replied, pulling out her tights, yoga top, and sneakers. "I need to get some fresh air."

"Mind if I join you?"

Angel turned to look at him curiously. "You run?" she asked.

"I'm a wolf," he answered snarkily.

"I meant on two legs," Angel replied. "I doubt the locals would appreciate a giant wolf running down the street."

"Good point," he admitted, "and I really should go talk to some of the other Alphas while I've got the time. You going to come downstairs for dinner?"

"I'll probably just order room service," Angel replied, starting to pull off her clothes.

"Alright," Caleb said, coming to stand in front of her, "I'll see you later, then." He leaned down and kissed her softly. "Have a good run."

"Thanks," Angel replied.

Caleb was gone for a few minutes before Angel realized she was standing half-dressed in the middle of the room, staring at the door and grinning like a fool. Shaking herself, she finished pulling on her running clothes, tucked the hotel key card into the pocket on the back of her shirt, and headed out.

CHAPTER 22

Caleb almost turned around and went back to the room at least three times before he reached the elevator. He wanted to spend every free second with Angel, but he was worried about crowding her and scaring her away again. So, as much as he wanted to go back to their hotel room, strip her naked, and spend the rest of the evening fucking her until she couldn't walk straight, he stepped into the elevator and pressed the button for the lobby. The shiny metal doors closed slowly, and with a jolt the elevator began to descend. Caleb reached the lobby and took a look around. He saw several Alphas he should probably talk to while they were here, but he decided he needed some time to himself before he dove back into work. He headed to the bar, got a beer, and parked himself in a booth near the back, where he was less likely to be disturbed.

He wasn't sure if having sex with Angel had made him more or less confused about his feelings towards her. Before, there'd always been this nagging doubt in his mind that his obsession with her was only because she'd essentially turned him down. Caleb could admit to himself that he had a bit of an ego - he was an Alpha male, after all - and sometimes that ego made him do stupid things. But if that had been the case, he would have slept with her once, rocked her world, and felt perfectly fine just walking away. At this point, though, Caleb didn't want to walk away. Angel suited him so damn well - both inside and outside the bedroom. She was strong in both body and mind, she protected those she cared for, even to the point of risking her own life, and she was a demon in the sack. Caleb hadn't enjoyed himself so much with a woman ever before, and he had no doubt in his mind she felt the same way.

The question, then, was why he couldn't figure out if she was his Mate or not. He'd never had a Mate before, but from what he'd heard from others, when a wolf met his or her Mate, there wasn't any uncertainty. Hell, he'd heard of wolves that had met and Mated without even knowing each other's names. Before he'd left for the conference, Caleb had spoken to Sara about his confusion. Females seemed to discuss these kinds of things a little more freely than males, so he'd been hoping she might have something helpful to tell him.

"I knew the first time I met Wyatt, he was my Mate," Sara had told him. "But I know lots of people who were friends or acquaintances with someone for months, or even years, before they realized they were their Mate. I think sometimes one or both people aren't quite ready to be Mated yet, which is why it sometimes takes a while for people to figure it out."

Sara's words had reassured him a little, making him think maybe, eventually something would just click and he'd know for sure whether Angel was his Mate or not. But she was a witch - did they even believe in soul mates? And if they did, could they sense it as easily as wolves could? Would Angel even want to be his Mate? He took a deep breath and blew it out, trying to settle his thoughts. He was getting ahead of himself. Angel had spent the last few months trying in vain to avoid him, for reasons he still didn't know. If she'd been so hesitant just to get involved with him, bringing up the idea that she might be his Mate would certainly send her running in the opposite direction. He had to tread carefully, lest he lose her for good.

"You look like a man deep in thought," Jesse told him, sliding into the seat across from him.

"Mmmhmm," Caleb grunted, still caught up in his thoughts.

"I'm guessing it has something to do with your witch?" Jesse asked.

"Mmmhmm."

"She's pretty cool, actually," Jesse said, "not nearly as stuck up as some other witches I've met. Do you think she really knows how to use those swords?"

"I don't doubt it," Caleb said proudly.

"You got it bad, Caleb," Jesse informed him.

Caleb shrugged, deciding he'd rather not share his internal struggle with the other wolf. Unfortunately for him, Jesse was very perceptive.

"You worried 'cause she's not a wolf?" Jesse asked.

"Not at all," Caleb replied - and he meant it. He didn't care if he Mated a witch or a wolf, or even a human for that matter. He knew wolf-witch pairings were almost non-existent, but he figured that was likely because wolves and witches didn't really socialize that well, or that often. There were some wolves who believed in keeping bloodlines "pure" - refusing to mate outside of their species, but Caleb had no such reservations. A soul mate was a precious thing, and throwing them aside because they weren't born a wolf was something Caleb would never do.

"Then what's the problem?"

"I'm not sure she's my Mate," Caleb admitted.

Jesse scoffed and rolled his eyes. "She is," he told Caleb.

"What makes you so sure?"

"The way you look at her when you think no one's looking," Jesse explained, "and how much you smile when you're with her. Oh, and the way you nearly ripped off my arm for touching her this morning. I'd hate to see what you'd do to an unfriendly, unmated male who dared touch her."

"Depends."

"On what?"

"On whether there was anything left of the guy after Angel was done with him."

Jesse nodded thoughtfully. "Good point," he said, raising his beer for a toast. "To women - can't live with 'em, can't live without 'em."

Caleb chuckled at the overused expression but tapped his bottle against Jesse's anyway.

CHAPTER 23

Angel woke just as the sun was rising and found herself wrapped in Caleb's arms, his nose buried in the crook of her neck. He was still sleeping; his even breaths tickled her skin, and she could feel how completely relaxed he was lying next to her. It made Angel wonder if maybe he had some inkling that they were Mates. She'd read Alpha males had an especially hard time relaxing around people who aren't family; their human sides might relax, but the wolf would still remain alert.

Glancing at the clock, Angel saw they still had about two hours before the conference started for the day. Turning so she was facing Caleb, Angel reached her hands up, tracing his lips, then the curve of his jawline. Feeling brave, she let her hands wander further; down to his chest, she skimmed her palms against his pecs and abs, the fine hairs tickling her skin. As she reached lower, Angel sensed a change in his breathing; he was awake now, but he kept his eyes closed. Leaning closer, Angel pressed a kiss to his collarbone, working her way up his throat, trailing kisses as she went. She took his earlobe into her mouth, sucking gently, and he tightened his arms around her. She chuckled.

"Good morning."

"With a wake up like that, it most certainly is," he replied, opening his eyes and trailing his hand down her arm.

"How were your meetings last night?" Angel asked, stretching her arms over head, thoroughly enjoying the patterns he was drawing on her skin with his finger.

"Far too long," Caleb replied, pulling her underneath him. She could feel his cock pressing against her thigh, and she arched her back to press her breasts against his chest. He growled deep in his throat. "Angel," he cautioned.

"I've already told you," she reminded him, "I'm not nearly as fragile as you think."

"And I'm not always as gentle as I seem," he told her, sliding his knee between her legs.

"Prove it," Angel goaded him, wanting to see what he was like when he really let himself go.

Instead of responding to her prodding, Caleb leaned forward, kissing her gently but passionately. All thoughts abandoned her, and Angel wrapped her arms around his neck, returning his kiss just as passionately. He grabbed the hem of her shirt and pulled it up over her head, then pulled off her panties. He sat back to admire the view for a moment, then leaned forward, taking a nipple into his mouth. Angel arched her back at the feeling, burying her fingers in his hair while he teased her with his mouth and tongue. Before too long, Angel was beyond ready to have him inside her. Pulling gently on his hair, she made him face her.

"Pants off," she demanded. He grinned at her, complying quickly, but when he climbed back onto the bed, he hesitated when she sat up and moved away from him. "Lie on your back," she told him.

He hesitated - he probably wasn't used to taking orders - but as he lay on his back, Angel could have sworn he was even more turned on than before. Straddling his waist, Angel took his cock in her hand, guiding it gently and lowering herself onto it slowly. He groaned out loud as she took his whole length inside her, reaching for her hips. She slapped away his hands.

"Nope," she scolded, "it's my turn now."

Caleb had never enjoyed doing what other people told him to do, but when Angel gave him orders, he was more than happy to obey. Even more surprising, he found the fact that she was taking charge incredibly arousing. But he wasn't going to admit that to her - at least not in so many words.

"You do realize bossing an Alpha around is not generally a good idea, right?" he asked, his voice thick with lust.

Angel rocked her hips, forward, then back, and his whole body tensed.

"I do," she replied, "but I'll take my chances."

Before he could reply, she started moving again, rocking her hips forward and back, sliding herself up and down. She varied the pace - first slow, then fast, then slow again - until he was clenching his jaw to keep from shouting out loud. She felt so damn good riding his cock, and the view of her breasts bouncing up and down would be burned into his memory for the rest of his life. Fighting his Alpha tendencies, Caleb had to grip the mattress to keep from flipping her over and taking control. He knew she probably wouldn't care if he took control, but he desperately wanted to see this to its glorious end. After what seemed like mere seconds, her whole body tensed, and she came quickly, tightly squeezing his cock. She cried out, flinging her head back, and his orgasm slammed into him suddenly. He growled, pushing his hips upward and grabbing her hips. After a minute or so, Angel collapsed against his chest, breathing heavily. He wrapped his arms around her, pulling her close.

"Okay," he admitted, "that was definitely a good idea."

CHAPTER 24

After the rather spectacular start to her day, very little could bother Angel. As expected, Matt was still a jerk, Jesse was still entertaining, and all the wolves attending the conference watched with varying degrees of suspicion. Much like the first day, she alternated between perimeter sweeps and bodyguard duty for Jonathan. Caleb stole her away for lunch again, and despite the strange looks they were getting from his fellow wolves, he was surprisingly affectionate with her.

"Cut it out, you two," Jesse teased, grabbing a chair and joining them. "All that mushy stuff is going to make me hurl."

"Then don't watch," Caleb told him, "problem solved."

"Easier said than done," Jesse said. "Anyway, you two coming to the gym tonight?"

"Gym?" Angel asked.

"Yeah," Jesse said, "gives everyone a chance to work off any extra energy or aggression."

Angel gave Caleb a quick look, wondering why he hadn't bothered to tell her about the gym.

"First I've heard of it," she told Jesse, "but I'm guessing it might not be a good idea for me to go."

"Nonsense," Jesse exclaimed, "you'll be fine. Between Caleb, me, and my dad, no one will bother you. Besides, Caleb keeps going on and on about your fighting skills. I wanna see what the fuss is all about."

"Not a chance," Caleb told him. The finality in his tone rubbed Angel the wrong way, so she ignored him.

"You want to fight me?" Angel asked Jesse.

"Yeah," Jesse replied. "I mean, I did, but Caleb doesn't seem too keen on the idea."

"Last I checked, Caleb wasn't the boss of me," Angel remarked. "I'm in. Where and when?"

Jesse grinned. "Excellent," he said. "We're planning on going after dinner, so just meet us out front, and we'll all go together."

"I'll be there."

"You're not seriously going to fight him, are you?" Caleb asked as Jesse left them alone.

"Why not?" Angel replied. "It's just a friendly sparring match."

"He's a wolf," Caleb explained, "and he's a damn good fighter."

"So am I," Angel told him, "and I'm a witch, too, so I think I'll be just fine."

Caleb huffed once, then ran a hand through his hair. "I'm not going to be able to talk you out of this, am I?"

"Nope."

"Fine, but I'm going with you."

"Okay."

Despite the fact that Caleb still tried to convince her not to go, they met up with Jesse and Jonathan after dinner. Jonathan explained that they had rented an empty warehouse just down the street, so they walked the short distance, arriving at the large, well-lit building in minutes.

Angel wasn't sure what she'd been expecting, but when they walked inside, she was thoroughly impressed with what she saw. There were ten sparring rings set up, complete with thick mats laid out on the concrete floor, and a row of punching bags along one wall.

"Wow," Angel told Jesse, "this is pretty cool."

"And necessary," Jonathan told her, "wolves don't do well stuck inside for too long."

At the far end of the building, near the other entrance, she noticed Matt berating a pair of wolves who were in various states of undress. The large open space made it easy for them to hear what he was saying.

"The rules are clear - no shifting and running loose. If you can't manage a week without shifting, you shouldn't be here."

One of the offenders seemed to think it was a good idea to try and argue. "But –"

"No buts." Matt's tone was deadly serious. "You've lost gym privileges for the rest of the week. If you have a problem with any of the rules, you can go right ahead and take it up with Alpha Pike."

The two wolves glanced nervously in Jonathan's direction for just a moment, then gathered up the rest of their clothes and scurried off.

"No shifting?" Angel asked, looking to Jonathan.

"We decided it was too risky," he explained. "It's not common for the conference, but it's necessary on occasion. Everyone will manage."

She nodded. It made sense - if everyone shifted and went for a run, it would be easy for vampires and zombies to pick them off one by one.

"C'mon, Angel," Jesse beckoned, motioning to one of the empty sparring rings, "we can grab a ring before it gets too busy."

"I still don't like this idea," Caleb announced.

"Relax, Caleb," Angel patted his arm reassuringly, "Jesse isn't going to hurt me."

"He most certainly will not," Caleb insisted, giving Jesse a meaningful glare.

"Seriously?" Angel exclaimed loudly. "This Alpha male, overprotective bullshit is getting annoying." Caleb gave her a meaningful look. "Alright, how about this," she began, "you can spar with me first."

"How would that help anything?" Caleb asked.

"Because," Angel explained, "then you would know for certain I can hold my own against a wolf, and you won't be so worried about Jesse hurting me - even by accident."

Caleb seemed to consider her suggestion for a moment,

but Angel had noticed the flash of wolf in his eyes and the way his scent changed. He was definitely going to say yes, he just didn't want her to realize how much her suggestion had excited him.

"Alright," Caleb said, with a nod.

"I'd tell you not to go easy on me, but I know I'd just be wasting my breath," Angel said, sitting down on the mat and removing her shoes.

"I have nearly a foot, and probably a hundred pounds on you," Caleb told her, "ignoring the fact that I'm a wolf, you'd still be outmatched. Of course I'm going to go easy on you."

"Outmatched?" Angel repeated, a wry smile turning up her mouth on one side. "If you say so."

Angel set her shoes and socks to the side, then pulled off her sweater. She was wearing workout clothes - yoga pants, sports bra, and T-shirt - all in black. Stepping onto the mat, she did a few quick stretches while Caleb removed his shoes, then his shirt. She tried not to think about how yummy he looked in just a pair of sweatpants, but it was tricky. Caleb must have noticed her watching him, because he winked at her and laughed.

"If you want," he said, "we could always go back to the hotel and get our exercise another way."

Angel blushed, and Jesse faked retching from the side of the mat.

"Please tell me this isn't going to turn into some sort of love fest - because if it is, the both of you should just take it outside."

Angel stuck out her tongue at him, then took up a fighter's stance: arms up, feet shoulder width apart, balanced on the balls of her feet. Caleb mimicked her pose, and they began to circle each other. She tried to focus, to remember the times she'd seen him fight before. Unfortunately, Angel hadn't really seen Caleb fight in his human form, which left her with very little to work with. The obvious place to start would be using his size against him - larger fighters tended just to plow through their opponents instead of being more skilled. Larger fighters were also usually slower, and less flexible.

Figuring she could use her speed to feel him out and get a better sense of his fighting style, Angel darted forward, feinting a right hook. Caleb dodged easily, stepping back and circling around to her left side. He kicked out with his right leg, but he pulled it back before it made contact, throwing himself slightly off balance. Angel saw her opening and took it, striking his side with her fist, jumping around him, and landing another punch to his back.

Caleb grunted slightly at the impact but quickly regained his balance and turned to face her. He reached out with one hand, grabbing for her arm, but she spun quickly and landed a hard kick to the back of his thigh. He turned quickly, sweeping out his leg to try and knock her off her feet. Angel dodged the leg, but he managed to wrap a hand around her upper arm, pulling her towards him. She struck - hard and fast - with her free arm, landing blows on his nose, sternum, and stomach. At the same time, her heel slammed down on the top of his foot. He released her quickly, stepping back and inhaling sharply, pressing the heel of his palm to his nose. Angel was pretty sure she'd broken it but wasn't too worried since she knew wolves could heal something like that in minutes. Reaching up with his other hand, Caleb wiggled his nose slightly, putting it back in place.

"That kinda hurt," he said matter-of-factly.

"Still wanna go easy on me?" Angel asked.

He didn't answer, just resumed his stance. They circled each other again, and this time Caleb made the first move. He swung his first forward, aiming for her shoulder; Angel started to dodge the blow out of reflex before deciding it might be better if he was able to get past his fear of hurting her. Stepping forward slightly, she took the hit. The force was enough to knock her back a step, but he was clearly pulling his punches. Not wanting to give him a chance to second-guess his actions, Angel stepped forward, landing several blows to his torso. Caleb stumbled back slightly, and Angel swore she could pinpoint the moment he decided going easy on her was a bad idea. He feinted left, then charged her, ducking her defensive punches, grabbing her upper arm, and pulling her off balance. Before she was able to regain her footing, Caleb circled behind her, wrapping his arms around her torso and pinning Angel's arms to her sides. She struggled for a moment, testing his grip, but it was pretty solid.

"Give up?" Caleb whispered in her ear.

"Fat chance," Angel replied haughtily.

After that, the sparring match was much more fun. Caleb stopped trying to baby her, and she got to show off her skills. Eventually, they called it a draw, and Jesse replaced Caleb for another match. Sparring with Jesse was a different kind of fun; he had less hand-to-hand combat training, but his instincts were still good. Eventually, when they were both breathing heavily and sweating, they wrapped up their match and left the mat to someone else. Caleb handed her a bottle of water and towel, smiling warmly and wrapping his arm around her shoulder.

"I'm sorry I doubted your abilities," he told her, "you're a pretty good fighter."

"You, too," Angel replied, winking at him.

They found a reasonably quiet place to sit and watch some of the other sparring matches, and the general flow of people coming and going. Several of the matches got heated, drawing large crowds. Most of them ended safely on their own, but at least one had to be broken up by Jonathan. A few hours after their arrival, they decided to head back to the hotel, so they texted Jesse to let him know they were leaving and walked out into the cool night air. They made it a short way down the road when familiar voices caught their attention.

"Look," Matt said, "I'm just trying to keep everyone safe. Jonathan won't discuss it with me any further, but maybe if you talk to him, he'll reconsider."

"This is just because she's a witch, Matt. You have no idea what she's capable of."

"Regardless of what she is, that's exactly the problem," Matt insisted. "She's an unknown variable, and I can't be certain of my security plans with her in the mix."

They turned a corner, and both males fell silent as they realized who had walked up on their conversation. Matt frowned at them, and Jesse looked apologetic.

"Let's go," Caleb said, trying to urge her forward.

"No."

"Don't worry about it, Angel," Jesse told her, but she held up her hand to stop him.

"It's fine." She turned to face Matt. "I actually agree with you on your last point."

"You do?"

"You do?" Caleb parroted.

"If I was at work and they told me I could pick a team to work with but kept sending random agents I knew nothing about to work with me, I'd be frustrated, too. It's hard to put yourself in a dangerous situation when you don't know if your team can even take care of themselves."

Matt crossed his arms, looking smug.

"So you'll leave?"

"Nope." Angel gave him a grin. "We're going to fight, and I'm going to prove to you I'm not a liability. Let's go."

She turned on her heel and headed back to the warehouse, the wolves hot on her heels. Caleb pulled her to a stop a few feet from the door, concern showing on his face.

"Are you sure about this?"

"Yes."

"Matt's not going to pull any punches."

"Neither am I." She squeezed his hand reassuringly. "Trust me."

Caleb hesitated a moment, then nodded and released her arm.

"Okay," he said. "Don't make me regret this."

They headed inside, and Jesse quickly commandeered a ring. Matt pulled off his shoes and shirt, stretching slightly.

"Terms?" he asked.

"Match goes until someone yields or someone can't continue."

"Agreed. Stakes?"

"If you win, I'll leave in the morning. If I win, you'll pay for my new blades."

"Fine." He turned and headed for the center of the ring.

Angel pulled off her shoes and stretched quickly, noticing they were already drawing a crowd. Just as she was about to step onto the mat, Caleb leaned in close and whispered in her ear.

"Be careful," he told her.

"I will," Angel replied, pressing a quick kiss to his cheek.

They faced off on the mat, and as Angel expected, Matt attacked first. Angel dodged, taking advantage of her small size to avoid his fists. She stayed on the defensive at first, getting a good sense of his fighting style, and any potential weaknesses. He was trained in a few forms of martial arts - Angel could see different elements of wrestling and karate - and he wasn't the kind of opponent you could wait out and strike when he grew tired. But Angel had just as much endurance as he did, and while she wasn't as strong, she was stronger than he thought, and that wasn't even counting her magic.

Nearly every wolf in the building was watching them now, and it was so quiet, you could almost hear a pin drop. Everyone seemed thoroughly intrigued at the idea of a fight between a wolf and a witch, and Angel had no doubt some of them were hoping for a bloodbath. For a moment, she questioned her decision to challenge Matt, but she quickly pushed aside those thoughts. Wolves respected strength, and the only way Matt, and many of the other wolves, would respect her was if she earned it.

Steeling herself, Angel went on the offensive. She charged forward, ducking his arms and landing several blows to his ribcage. Hopping backwards, she caught a glancing blow to her shoulder; it stung, but it wasn't anything she could handle. Angry that she'd managed to strike him, Matt upped his game. He drove her backwards with an aggressive attack, but

Angel was ready for him. Intentionally dropping her guard, she savored the look on his face as he realized he was going to land a solid punch. She then teleported behind him and delivered a spinning kick to his lower legs.

Matt stumbled slightly, then turned to face her, a look of confusion on his face. It passed quickly, and once again he was on the attack. Angel attacked as well, teleporting mere inches to avoid his fists and landing a strong right hook to his jaw.

They continued like this for a while - Matt attacking aggressively, and Angel using her recently perfected teleporting ability to get the upper hand. He quickly realized she was using magic against him, but there was nothing he could do about it. Instead, he slowed his attacks and started trying to trick her. He would feint left and go right or purposely drop his guard to try and lure her into his reach. Angel managed to hold her own for a while, but eventually he caught her. Matt grabbed her from behind, wrapping his arms around her tightly, pinning her arms. Angel struggled a bit, testing his grip, but it was solid.

"Yield," Matt demanded.

Angel ignored him, and he squeezed her tighter. Her breath left her in a whoosh, and her ribs ached with the pressure. A growl came from the crowd, and Angel looked up to see Caleb standing in front of her. He was not happy. His eyes glowed brightly, and she could see a fine layer of fur had erupted on his arms.

Angel flashed Caleb a quick thumbs up, and he seemed to calm somewhat. She then returned her focus to Matt. Gripping his forearms in her hands, Angel lifted her feet off the ground, as if she were going to try and throw him over her shoulder. As expected, Matt leaned back to counter her weight. Moving quickly, Angel reversed her movement, throwing up her legs and propelling her body over his shoulders. As she completed the flip, she braced her knees and brought her heels down on the backs of his legs. The blow was harsh, and the movement unexpected, and Matt went down hard, sprawling face first on the floor. Moving quickly, Angel jumped on his back and bent one arm behind him at an awkward angle.

"Yield," she demanded.

Matt growled at her, struggling against her hold, and Angel tightened her grip, bending his arm even further. He growled again, louder this time, and Angel had very little warning before he bucked her off and swiped at her with a clawed hand. Apparently, his wolf was none too happy about getting beat up by a witch. His change was completed in seconds, and now she faced a very large - very angry - grey wolf.

"Angel!" Caleb called out, stepping forward to try and get between her and Matt.

"Don't!" Angel shouted, holding out her hand to stop him.

Keeping one eye on Matt, Angel saw Caleb hesitate, then step back slowly. His eyes blazed brightly, and his lips were pressed together in a tight line. He was not happy, but he was trusting that she could take care of herself. Turning her full attention to Matt, she took a deep breath, trying to calm her racing heart. She had been hoping things wouldn't get this far, but now that they had, she had to end it quickly. Her own wolf was already itching to be let loose so she could show this big, dumb male who was stronger. That was something Angel definitely wasn't ready for. She moved, slowly at first, circling Matt, assessing his mood. When he'd first changed, Angel had assumed it had been involuntary - that he'd been angry about her pinning him. Looking closely, it seemed she had been wrong. The wolf was calm, watching her closely, baring his teeth menacingly. The idiot was trying to scare her into submission.

"Did you really think that would work, Matt?" she asked him, relaxing her stance and putting her hands on her hips. "Like I haven't been around a big ass wolf before?"

The wolf watched her for a moment, curious, before charging towards her, snapping and snarling. Angel teleported across the mat, and he turned quickly, watching her again.

"Very scary," Angel mocked, "I can hardly contain myself."

"What the hell are you doing?" Jesse hissed at her from the sidelines.

"Poking the bear," Angel replied casually.

Matt charged again, and again Angel teleported out of his way. Turning to face her, he growled loudly, bared his teeth, and crouched low. He leapt at her, and this time Angel didn't teleport out of his way. She faced him and watched the look of triumph spread across his face as he flew through the air.

"That's more than enough, I think," Angel told him, holding up her hand just before Matt reached her. He stopped in mid-air, then rose upwards until he was hovering fifteen feet above the mat. He glared down at her, growling in what Angel assumed was a demand to be put down. Glancing out at the wolves who had gathered to watch the fight, Angel saw a wide range of reactions. Some people were laughing at Matt, some appeared impressed at her abilities, and some seemed angry.

"Whoa," Jesse exclaimed, "I didn't know you could do that." He turned to Caleb. "Did you know she could do that?"

"Uh, no, not really," Caleb replied, looking just as surprised as everyone else.

A loud growl brought her focus back to the task at hand. Matt was not happy; he struggled in mid-air, trying to free himself. When he was unsuccessful, he shifted, and within seconds he was in his human form again - naked now - and still stuck. He stared her down, his gaze calculating.

"How long can you hold me up here?"

She shrugged. "Long enough. Ready to admit I've won?"

"What if I break your concentration? Would the spell fail?"

"Potentially. But I've got a lot of practice using magic in stressful situations, so you'd probably have to injure me to manage it, and I'm pretty sure you're unarmed at the moment."

She grinned at him and heard numerous chuckles from the crowd. Matt eyed her thoughtfully, then nodded.

"I yield."

Angel lowered him to the ground slowly, and someone tossed him a pair of sweatpants. He pulled them on, then stepped towards her.

"Not bad," he said, holding out his hand.

"Is that the best I'm going to get?"

He shrugged, but Angel was pretty sure she saw a hint of amusement in his eyes. She reached out and shook his hand firmly.

"You're different than most witches I've met," he said.

"Let me guess," Angel replied, "you're used to the 'I'm better than everyone else' kind of witch?"

"Yep."

"I hate those people."

Matt considered her for a moment before nodding. "I'm not too proud to admit when I'm wrong," he said, "and it seems I was wrong about you."

"Glad to hear it."

CHAPTER 25

"Good morning, little witch," Caleb whispered into Angel's ear.

"Morning," she mumbled, rubbing sleep from her eyes. She looked so damn adorable first thing in the morning; Caleb found himself grinning like an idiot. He was doing that a lot lately.

"Sleep well?"

"Yeah," she replied, stretching so she rubbed against him in the most wonderful way. "How about you?"

"I slept okay," he told her. "To be honest, I was still a little tense after your fight with Matt."

"You thought I was gonna get my butt kicked, didn't you?" Angel teased.

"No," Caleb replied, pushing himself up to look down at her, "I thought you were going to get yourself killed. But you definitely proved me wrong. You were holding back when you were sparring with me and Jesse."

"Yeah, I was," she admitted, "but I didn't have anything to prove to you or Jesse. I needed to prove to Matt that I could handle myself, or he would have given me a hard time for the rest of the week."

"Sometimes I'm surprised at how well you understand wolves."

"It's not like the information isn't readily available to anyone who wants to learn. Besides, me knowing more about wolves means I don't get weirded out when you do things like cover me in your scent before I leave the hotel room."

"You noticed that, huh?" Caleb asked, worried that, despite her arguments to the contrary, his behavior had made her feel uncomfortable.

"Of course I noticed!" Angel exclaimed. "But I know it means you care enough to warn other males away from me, so I don't really mind."

Caleb smiled widely and reached out a hand, gently caressing her cheek. "I do care," he told her, "I care very much. You mean a great deal to me."

Angel blinked rapidly, then turned her head so he couldn't see her face. Her body tensed next to his, and Caleb could smell the change in her mood. She was surprised, a little happy, and coming through strongest was the scent of fear. He should have expected that, given her previous reluctance to let him get close, but it bothered him that he caused her to be afraid. She could take on pissed off wolves and crazy black witches without a second thought, but personal relationships scared her deeply.

"Talk to me," he urged, brushing the hair back from her face. "Why does me admitting I care scare you so much?"

"I'm not good at this kind of thing," she answered.

"You've told me that before," he pressed, "elaborate."

Angel sighed, then sat up in the bed, wrapping a blanket around herself. Caleb stayed where he was, giving her time to think. She stayed silent for a few minutes, and Caleb was beginning to worry he'd pushed too much when she finally began.

"I've always had a hard time trusting people," she explained. "People lie, they try to manipulate you, they let you down. It's easier just to not expect anything, because then you won't be disappointed."

"That's a little bleak," Caleb noted.

"And lonely," Angel added. She fell silent again, staring at her hands in her lap.

"There's something else, isn't there?" Caleb asked.

"I -" Angel began but snapped her mouth shut. "There are...things about myself I keep secret. Things I've never told anyone, because I'm afraid of what people will think. Or say. Or do."

"I will never hurt you," Caleb assured her, reaching out and resting his hand on her shoulder.

"Maybe not intentionally," Angel said, "but without knowing my secrets, you can't make that promise."

"I couldn't–"

"I'm in love with you," she said, making eye contact for a moment before dropping her gaze back to her lap.

Caleb took a moment to let her words sink in, to understand what it meant, and to evaluate his own feelings. He cared for her - more than he had cared for any other female before - but did he love her? His wolf was elated at her confession and urged his other half to reciprocate, but the beast still had no clear answer on whether Angel was their Mate. She was right - he might not want to cause her harm, but he could do it very easily. If she wasn't his Mate and Caleb committed himself to her, only to find his true Mate later on, it would devastate her. But he wasn't even sure she wasn't his true Mate! What if this was some kind of challenge for him to overcome? What if his wolf was being difficult on purpose, to see if he would be able to recognize his Mate on his own? It sounded crazy, but he was sick of not knowing. Here he had a strong, confident, beautiful woman who loved him, and he couldn't make up his damn mind.

"I–" he began, intending to return the sentiment, but she held up her hand to stop him.

"I can see the wheels turning up there," she said, tapping his forehead, "and I don't want you to say something you don't really mean. Think about it, and get back to me later, okay?"

Caleb wanted to argue with her, but she was right. He needed more time to think, and it wouldn't be fair to either of them if he spoke the words without really meaning them. Taking her hand in his, he brushed a kiss across her knuckles.

"You're amazing, you know that?"

She grinned at him. "I've been told so a couple times," she replied. She glanced at the clock, then leaned forward to plant a kiss on his cheek. "I'm going to take a shower, then head downstairs for breakfast. You should take some time for yourself today."

"I will," he said, watching appreciatively as she climbed out of bed and headed for the bathroom.

CHAPTER 26

Angel wouldn't say she rushed out of the hotel room, but she certainly didn't dawdle. When Caleb had pushed her to talk to him, she'd been so close to biting the bullet and telling him the truth. Instead, she'd chickened out and opted for a slightly less terrifying confession - that she loved him. When he hadn't responded immediately, she'd experienced so many emotions - joy, hope, fear, sadness, anger, embarrassment - in such quick succession, she felt like she was going to explode. Thankfully, her rational brain had caught up just in time to stop him from replying. While it made sense for him to think things over and get back to her later, Angel was planning on using that time to prepare for the worst. The last thing she wanted was to hear he didn't love her back and turn into a puddle in front of him and a hotel full of other wolves.

She entered the dining room, grabbed breakfast from the buffet, and claimed an empty booth against the wall. As she ate, she noticed something a little strange. Several of the wolves were watching her curiously while they ate, and a few even greeted her politely. When she went to grab another cup of coffee, the wolf ahead of her actually offered to pour her a fresh cup. She tried to ignore it, but it was just too weird after two days of being completely ignored or insulted behind her back. She was getting ready just to grab a couple pancakes and leave when Jesse flopped down in the seat across from her.

"Morning," he greeted.

"Morning," Angel replied distractedly.

"What's up?" Jesse asked, proving that while he may act like a goof, he wasn't completely oblivious.

"People are being nice to me," Angel told him.

"And?"

"Let me be clearer - wolves are being nice to me. All week they've been pretending I don't exist or throwing insults at me, or both - which really shouldn't be possible, but they still managed to find a way. What gives?"

"Oh, I see," Jesse said around a mouthful of toast. "It's because of your fight with Matt last night. A lot of people saw it, or heard about it from someone who was there. They're impressed; you managed to prove your worth without completely humiliating or injuring him."

"But I didn't prove myself against any of them."

"No, but not even an Alpha has to beat up everyone to prove he deserves to lead. You managed to win a challenge against a very strong, very skilled wolf, and you've earned their respect."

"Whatever," Angel said, shaking her head. "I like to think I've got most of this pack stuff figured out, but apparently I still have a lot to learn."

"Yep," Jesse agreed. "Don't worry about it. You understand more than most."

"So I've been told."

"Look on the bright side," Jesse told her, "you probably won't have to deal with any more bigoted wolves this week."

"True," Angel acknowledged. "So, anything special on the agenda for today?"

"Not really. More meetings."

"Well," Angel admitted, "I suppose it's better than the alternative."

The day went fairly smoothly - or as smoothly as things can go at a werewolf conference. There was the occasional shouting/growling match, but Jonathan always managed to intervene before it got violent and calm everyone down. Angel had lunch with Jesse and a couple other wolves who were interested in meeting her. Most of them were actually quite nice. Matt still ignored her, only speaking to Jesse when he needed them to cover another meeting or do a perimeter check, but she was pretty sure he was still feeling a little cowed from the night before. She hadn't been expecting him to change completely overnight and happily gave him space. Before Angel knew it, the meetings were done for the day, and she was free to do as she pleased. She headed back to her hotel room for a little peace and quiet, and to figure out her plans for the evening.

The room was empty when she arrived, though Angel hadn't been expecting to see Caleb. Even though the formal meetings were done, a lot of the Alphas still had a lot of things to discuss together. Caleb would be busy late into the evening. Angel browsed the room service and takeout menus, deciding she didn't really feel like eating on her own tonight. Jesse and a few of the wolves she'd met at lunch had made plans to go to the hotel bar that evening, and they'd been nice enough to invite her. Angel contemplated leaving her weapons in the room but decided she'd rather keep the new - and expensive - blades with her at all times. She then headed downstairs.

It was only 7:30pm, but Jesse and several other wolves had already claimed a large table in the restaurant. Angel snagged a seat across from Jesse and between two of the wolves she'd met at lunch. Serguei was a long-limbed wolf with a strong Russian accent from Alberta who had been impressed with her hand-to-hand combat skills against Matt. Martin was a smaller wolf from the Montreal pack who fancied himself something of a ladies' man.

"Angel!" Jesse greeted her brightly. "You decided to join us after all."

"Why not?" Angel shrugged. "Drunk wolves are pretty darn entertaining."

"What's your poison?" Martin asked. "I think this place has a decent wine selection."

Angel resisted the urge to laugh in his face.

"Wine? No, thanks." She scoffed, then caught the waiter's attention, ordering a steak dinner and whiskey.

"Why does it not surprise me you're a whiskey girl?" Jesse asked.

"'Cause you're not as dumb as you look?" Angel suggested.

The table erupted in laughter at her jab, which - of course - Jesse handled gracefully.

"I can't imagine how much of me you can actually see from down there," he joked. "I mean, I suppose I could have a dumb looking belly button. I've never really checked."

"Oooh," Angel said, "a short joke. How original."

They talked and joked together, eating and drinking, for several hours. Angel enjoyed herself immensely; Jesse and the others were very entertaining. She got to hear all sorts of stories - some of which were most certainly fictional - and even shared a few of her own. By 11pm, several wolves said goodnight and headed for bed. After that, the group grew smaller and smaller as other people called it a night. It was just about midnight, and only Angel and Jesse were left at the bar when Caleb came looking for her.

"Here you are," he said, coming to sit next to her. "I was a little surprised when I didn't find you in bed already. It's pretty late."

"What're you, my mother?" Angel asked.

"Are you drunk?"

"Just a little buzzed," Angel admitted, grinning widely.

Hopping off her barstool, she pulled Caleb close and kissed him deeply. When she pulled back, he shot Jesse a harsh look.

"Don't blame me," Jesse said defensively. "I suggested she slow down, but she wouldn't listen."

"Just because I'm a witch, doesn't mean I'm a lightweight," Angel insisted.

"I never said you were," Caleb said, "but it's probably about time to head to bed. We've got another early morning."

"And someone wants to get some tonight," Jesse blurted out, slapping his hand against his mouth as soon as the words were out. Angel could see Caleb's wolf in his eyes and quickly stepped between the two of them.

"Hey now, Caleb," she said softly, resting her palms in his

chest, “it was just a joke. He didn’t–” She stopped suddenly, jolted by a thread of magic coming from the ward she’d set up around the hotel. Reaching out with her magic, Angel tried to get more information on what had triggered the ward.

“What is it?” Caleb asked, noticing the change in her demeanor.

“The ward’s been breached,” she replied. “At least three people without heartbeats, north of the hotel.”

Caleb was in motion instantly. “Jesse, you get your father. I’ll go get Matt.” He turned to face her. “Wait for us at the back door.”

He was gone a moment later, making use of his werewolf speed.

“Not likely,” Angel mumbled under her breath, keenly aware he might still actually hear her if she spoke at a normal volume.

“Uh, Angel,” Jesse began, but she held up a hand to stall him.

“I'm perfectly fine,” Angel told him, “just go get Jonathan, and I'll meet you out there.” Jesse seemed to think for a moment before nodding and heading for the door.

“You better not let Caleb tear me apart,” he told her, “‘cause you know he's going to try and blame me for ‘letting’ you go.”

“I won't,” Angel assured him.

She took a deep breath and downed a healing potion to help shake off the last of the alcohol. She then focused on the area of the ward that was breached and teleported to the field behind the hotel.

CHAPTER 27

Angel remained perfectly still, giving her eyes time to adjust to the darkness and – hopefully – not giving away her position to any of the trespassers. Making use of her other senses, she took a deep breath, catching the smell of pine trees and death. She didn't smell too much decay, which suggested the trespassers were vampires; zombies tended to rot pretty quickly after being created. She saw them now, three dark figures emerging from the tree line, moving slowly and quietly. They were headed towards the hotel, and they didn't seem to have noticed her yet. Moving quickly, she teleported behind them, waiting until they were right out in the open before catching their attention.

"Not sure if you got the memo," she said, startling them, "but this is a werewolf conference."

They turned to watch her, eyes darting around, looking around for more people. They looked young, both in body and spirit, and nervous. The one in the middle – she decided to call him Curly on account of his hair – inhaled deeply, scenting her, and his face scrunched up in confusion.

"A witch!?" he remarked. "They've got a witch guarding them?"

"Yep," Angel said brightly. "Now, if you don't mind, you're going to have to come with me. My employer is gonna want to ask you some questions."

"Yeah right," the one on the right – Blondie – scoffed. "You really think you scare us?"

Angel pulled her swords from behind her back.

"Probably not," she replied, "but I'm sure I can fix that."

They charged her all at once, and it was quickly apparent none of them had any experience in hand-to-hand combat. Unfortunately, they were still vampires, and vampires are faster and stronger than any other creature. She managed to duck punches from Curly and Blondie, but the third – Sideburns – caught her on the shoulder. Angel turned quickly, shaking off the blow and striking out with her blade, catching Sideburns on the forearm. He jumped back, cursing her as blood stained his shirt. Curly came at her next, wielding a sloppy right hook. Angel ducked, then swept out her leg, knocking his feet out from under him. He fell flat on his face, and she took the opening, jumping forward and jamming a sword through his stomach. It wouldn't kill him, but it would slow him down significantly.

Before she could pull the blade free, Blondie grabbed her from behind, wrapping his arms around her shoulders. Angel reacted on instinct, slamming her head back forcefully. He released her, and she turned to see he was clutching his broken nose. She reached for the blade embedded in Curly's stomach, but Sideburns landed a solid kick to her ribs before she could grab the handle. Angel fell to the ground, certain she had at least one cracked rib, but she couldn't stay down. Rolling, she came to her feet quickly, if painfully. Sideburns was charging her, and Blondie wasn't too far behind him. Hoping to keep them at bay until the wolves caught up, she made use of her teleportation abilities. Sideburns reached for her, and suddenly she was ten feet to his right. He snarled angrily and changed direction. Angel moved again, ending up behind both of them. Blondie – proving he wasn't nearly as dumb as he looked – motioned to Sideburns, and they moved to approach her from either side.

Angel mentally cursed – they might not be very skilled in fighting, but they did seem to have some amount of common sense. Crossing her fingers that the wolves would hurry their asses up and get there soon, she kept up her little game of cat-and-mouse. Each time, the vampires got closer, and Angel had to start teleporting near-blind to keep ahead of them.

She heard the wolves before she saw them. Howls rang out in the night, and Angel's wolf pushed to get to the surface, aching to fight the vampires with tooth and claw. She took a moment to regain control, but it was a moment too long. Sideburns slammed into her, and they both went down in a tangle of limbs. She ended up on her back, with the vampire on top of her. Her sword had slipped from her hand, leaving her weaponless. Sideburns pinned her arms to the ground, bared his fangs, and was pulled off her when a giant brown wolf collided with him. Moving quickly, Angel snatched up her sword and jumped to her feet. The brown wolf – Jesse, judging by the eyes – had Sideburns's right arm between his jaws, and the vampire was using his left to try and pry him off. A moment later, Caleb was at her side, still in human form.

"What the hell did I tell you!?" he shouted.

"Since when do I do what you tell me to do?" Angel shouted back.

Caleb opened his mouth to answer but closed it, clearly flummoxed. Before he had a chance to figure out a response, Blondie slammed into him. Caleb kept his feet, shoving away the vampire and lashing out with a strong left hook. A gray wolf dashed by them – Angel recognized Matt from the night before – and helped Jesse with Sideburns. Seeing the wolves had things well in hand, Angel went to retrieve her second sword and make sure Curly didn't go anywhere.

The injured vampire was lying on his side, clutching his belly and whimpering. Stomach wounds were supposed to be particularly unpleasant, and Angel was glad she hadn't had the pleasure of experiencing one herself. Watching Curly closely, just in case he was really good at faking it, Angel reached down and scooped up her sword. She took a few steps back so she could watch Curly and everyone else at the same time. Jesse and Matt had pretty much ripped Sideburns apart; apparently, he had decided to keep fighting, even though the smart thing to do would have been lying still and giving up. Caleb was still sparring with Blondie, though the vampire was looking a little worse for wear, with a new black eye and broken wrist.

Suddenly, Angel was on her back. Acting purely on instinct, she rolled and just managed to avoid the kick Curly was directing at her head. Jumping to her feet, she braced herself and held up her blades. Curly faced her, blood covering his front, fangs bared, and pissed.

"Stupid witch!" he spat.

"Bring it," Angel taunted, knowing she had a pretty decent chance at taking him down.

Curly snarled and charged her, ducking her blades and landing a solid punch to her stomach. Angel raised her knee, striking him in the groin; he stumbled back a step. Seeing an opening, Angel drove her sword through his left shoulder. The blade got stuck, so she left it, dancing back and circling behind him. He barely reacted to the new wound, turning so he could still watch her. Angel watched him, trying to gauge his next move. He was already moving slowly from the stomach injury, and while he was trying to appear unaffected by the sword in his shoulder, it was hurting him. He was angry, and unskilled, which meant he was projecting his next move. His right arm pulled back slightly, his shoulders pushed forward a few inches, he shifted his weight to his right foot. He was going to charge her and try for a right hook.

Angel braced herself, watching him closely, ready for him to make his move. With a shout, he launched himself forward, fisted his right hand, and pulled back his arm. She shifted her weight to her right foot, ready to dodge the blow and land a solid strike to his back that would definitely put him down for the night. Just before he reached her, Caleb slammed into Curly from the side, knocking him to the ground. The impact caused the blade in his shoulder to move, and the vampire screamed in pain.

"Okay, okay," Curly cried out. "I surrender. I surrender!"

Caleb handed him off to one of the wolves who'd just arrived, then moved quickly to stand in front of Angel. His hands skimmed over her gently, checking for injuries. Angel tolerated it briefly before pushing away his hands.

"Are you alright? Did he hurt you?" Caleb asked, continuing to touch her all over.

"Stop that," Angel told him, annoyed. "I'm fine."

"Are you sure?" Caleb insisted. "It looked like he hit you."

"In case you haven't noticed," Angel said angrily, "I can take a punch or two."

"Are you...mad at me?" Caleb asked, confused.

"Yes, I am!"

"Why?"

"I didn't need your help with that last vampire," she explained, gesturing to Curly. "I had everything under control."

"He hit you," Caleb said.

"Really?! I hadn't noticed," Angel replied sarcastically, retrieving the sword they'd pulled out of Curly and heading towards the hotel.

"What is your problem?" Caleb demanded.

Angel froze on the spot. He hadn't just asked her a question, he'd used his Alpha voice and demanded an answer. She could feel the weight of the command, and if she wasn't supposed to be his Mate, she'd be compelled to answer. Instead, it just made her angrier. She turned on her heel, walked forward until she was standing before him, and slapped him across the face.

"Don't you ever use that tone with me, ever again," she said, raising her voice enough that the other wolves paused to watch. "I am not one of your wolves. You cannot, and will not, order me around. As for my problem, it's with you, and your ridiculous mindset when it comes to females. You've seen me fight, you know what I'm capable of, and yet you still insist on interfering."

"Interfering?" Caleb repeated, scrunching up his face in confusion. "You were fighting a vampire! Of course I'm going to interfere. He could have killed you."

"But he wasn't going to. As I've already said, I had everything under control."

"I still don't see why you're so upset," Caleb told her.

Angel resisted the urge to slap him again for being so dense. She took a deep breath before replying.

"I am upset because despite having concrete proof that I can fight just as well – if not better than – you, and despite the fact that you recommended me for this job, you still don't really trust my abilities. I'm also upset because instead of asking me what was wrong, you ordered me to tell you."

"But I–" Caleb began, but she cut him off.

"Just please don't say anything else," Angel pleaded. "I can't promise I won't throw something at you if you say one more stupid thing." She took a deep breath, counted to five, and exhaled slowly. "I'm going back to the hotel, and I'm going to bed. You should find somewhere else to sleep tonight."

Caleb watched Angel walk away, completely at a loss for words. He'd interfered with her fight, yes, but he still didn't completely understand why it had upset her so much. The other part – him ordering her to tell her what was wrong – he could understand. Angel had an Alpha personality, and Alphas didn't like being ordered around. He stood there for a minute, processing what had just happened, until Jesse came up and patted him on the shoulder.

"For a minute there, I really thought she was gonna start using that sword on you," Jesse said. "She was really pissed off."

"I noticed," Caleb replied, absently rubbing the cheek she'd slapped.

"We're gonna bring these two somewhere a little more private," Jesse told him, indicating the two surviving vampires, "and see if we can't figure out why they decided to crash our party. Wanna come? Or do you need to work some damage control?"

Caleb considered going after her but eventually decided against it. Angry females were difficult to deal with at the best of times, and he wasn't used to dealing with non-wolf females. He needed more time to process what had happened and figure out how to fix things with Angel.

"I'll come with you," Caleb replied, "I think it might be best to give her time to cool down."

"Smart man," Jesse said. "Don't worry about it, you'll work things out; in the meantime, you can sleep on the couch in my room."

"Thanks."

CHAPTER 28

She watched closely from her vantage point, perched on top of a warehouse that was closed for the night. From here, she had an excellent view of the back of the hotel. She'd spotted movement in the forest only a few moments ago, so she knew it was only a matter of minutes before the show started. She sat silently, unmoving, waiting. She felt the surprising tingle of magic on her skin a few moments before three figures appeared on the hotel's back lawn. Another figure then appeared before them, almost instantly. From this distance, she could see it was a female. And she could feel her magic, even at this distance.

"A witch," she murmured to himself. "Interesting."

She watched, intrigued, as the vampires attacked. The witch pulled two short swords from beneath her jacket and met them head on. She fought well, using her magic to counter their speed. One went down quickly, but the other two managed to put her on the defensive. Just when things were getting interesting, several wolves arrived. Working together, they managed to take down the other vampires in only a few minutes. She watched as the wolves shifted and moved to take away the surviving vampires, likely to question them. She wasn't concerned. They didn't know anything.

She stood to leave, glad her little test had proved so informative. A witch working with the wolves was unexpected, but not a problem.

CHAPTER 29

The interrogation was less than helpful. The trespassing vampires weren't particularly brave, and within half an hour they'd told the wolves everything. Turns out, some random vampire had sent out an ad to some sort of vampire Craigslist, offering a decent amount of money for them just to walk up to the hotel. Of course, this generous soul had promised payment after they returned and hadn't told them they might encounter werewolves. Matt, Caleb, and Jesse tossed around the idea of letting them go and sending a few wolves to follow them when they tried to collect their payment, but in the end they decided it was highly unlikely whoever hired them would actually show up. Still, they weren't about to risk their captives revealing any information to outside sources, so they killed the vampires quickly and burned their bodies in the forest. A little brutal, maybe, but according to vampire laws, an unprovoked attack against the wolves meant their lives were forfeit.

It was nearing 2am by the time they headed back to the hotel. Caleb followed Jesse into his room, grabbed an extra blanket, and stretched out on the couch. Despite the late hour and earlier fight, sleep didn't come easy. His mind was running through his fight with Angel, at how upset she'd been, and at how poorly he'd handled the situation. He was used to protecting people, used to protecting females; it was hard-wired into his brain. Even female wolves, most of whom are completely capable of taking care of themselves, appreciated when a male stepped in to protect them.

But Angel was different. She was used to taking care of herself, of not having anyone to protect her. She'd proven herself more than once in Caleb's eyes, and while he really did trust her abilities, his instincts still pushed him to protect her. He needed to find a way to rein in his protective tendencies and explain them better to Angel, or this kind of situation was likely to happen again. But first he needed to come up with a suitable apology.

He was pretty sure Angel wasn't a flower or poetry person; chocolates didn't really seem like her thing either. Caleb racked his brain, trying to think of what he could do to make it up to her. Shortly after 3am, an idea struck him suddenly, and it was perfect. He fell asleep quickly then, a smile on his face, certain he wouldn't be sleeping on Jesse's couch for more than one night.

Angel was having a terrible time getting to sleep. When she'd first returned to the hotel room, she'd been fuming, taking out her anger and frustration on various items she could easily throw around. But now, lying in the dark, without Caleb beside her for the first time all week, she was lonely. She seriously considered tracking him down and inviting him back to their room, but her pride – and her wolf – wouldn't let her. If things were going to work out between them, Caleb needed to get over his intense need to protect her.

Eventually – hopefully – Angel would go back to work, and what would happen then? Would Caleb or one of his wolves follow her around, making sure she was safe? No. That wasn't a scenario Angel was even willing to consider. She needed to be firm with him about this now, or else there would be no stopping his overprotective tendencies when it came to her. She'd wait until the next day and find some time for them to talk things over. In the meantime, she had to figure out some way of turning off her overactive brain and going to sleep. Repositioning her pillow for the umpteenth time, she turned onto her side, took a deep breath, and tried to relax.

CHAPTER 30

"Are you sure continuing with this conference is a good idea?"

Melanie, his mate, sounded worried. He'd called her despite the late hour to let her know about their uninvited guests and assure her he and Jesse were safe.

"At this point, I don't have much choice," he replied. "If these threats are legitimate, whoever sent those vampires must be watching. If they see us getting ready to leave, who knows what they'll do?"

"You may be right, Jonathan," she said, "but that doesn't mean I'm happy about this whole situation."

"I know, Mel," he told her, "and for the record, I never said I was happy with it either."

"Be safe," she said.

"I will," he promised.

He ended the call and set his cell phone on the coffee table. While he wouldn't call what happened tonight an attack, he certainly saw it for what it was: a test. Whoever was responsible wanted to see how strong their defenses were. It was a smart strategy; send in someone disposable, sit back, and watch closely. It gave their enemy the chance to gather information, and it gave them absolutely nothing.

Snatching up his phone, he scrolled through his contacts until he came to the one he wanted. The phone rang twice before someone answered.

"Hello," came a curt but polite female voice from the other end of the line.

"This is Master Alpha Jonathan Pike," he replied, "I want to speak to Clan Leader Andrew."

“Leader Andrew is busy at the moment,” the receptionist began, but Jonathan cut him off.

“Three vampires attacked my conference tonight,” he said sharply. “I will speak to Andrew, and I will speak to him now.”

“One moment, sir,” she replied.

The line fell silent for less than a minute before Andrew picked up.

“Master Alpha Pike,” Andrew answered, his voice smooth and almost slippery sounding, a common trait among very old vampires.

“Clan Leader Andrew,” Jonathan replied. “Why do I have vampires gatecrashing my conference?”

“I have no idea,” Andrew told him plainly.

“I find that difficult to believe.”

“Do you know what every wolf in the country is doing right now?” Andrew asked. “I can’t imagine you do. In much the same way, we do not know what every vampire in the country is doing at a given time. We regret the actions of the individuals that encroached on your territory. I assume they have been dealt with?”

“They have.”

“And were you able to question them regarding their motives?”

“We were.” Jonathan paused, unsure whether he should share information when the Clan Leaders weren’t exactly doing the same. He quickly decided the information wasn’t useful enough to keep to himself. “They were hired anonymously to visit the hotel. From what we can tell, they didn’t know why, or who hired them.”

“If you’re willing to provide the information they gave you, we can certainly look into the incident,” Andrew offered, but it was an empty gesture. They’d offered to look into the threats against the conference but had told him nothing. Either they knew and weren’t interested in sharing information, or they were just as in the dark as he was.

"I'm certain we can look into it ourselves," Jonathan told him, trying to maintain a neutral tone.

"Very well," Andrew replied.

A moment later, the line went dead. Jonathan scowled at the phone a moment before setting it back down. It didn't surprise him the vampires were still being unhelpful. He just wished he had a better idea of where they stood.

CHAPTER 31

Alice was hungry. It had been nearly two days since she'd been fed, but it felt like it had been months. Her stomach cramped, and her mouth felt so very dry. The others like her were suffering the same way. But it could be worse. She glanced over at the Quiet Ones - the name they'd given to the inhuman creatures with vacant eyes - and shuddered involuntarily. They were hungry, too, and while they didn't move unless they were told to, she'd seen firsthand what happened when someone got too close. A man in a tattered jogging suit had approached one of them, trying to figure out what they were, and as soon as he was within reach, they'd descended on him like a pack of wild dogs. The sound of his screams would haunt Alice forever. Or maybe not. She'd heard their handlers talking a few hours ago, and while she didn't fully understand what was going on, she got the impression they'd be moving again soon. She also got the impression most of them weren't expected to survive what was coming next. Alice wasn't sure if she should be afraid or grateful.

CHAPTER 32

Caleb woke early Thursday morning with a pretty nasty crick in his neck. Hotel couches weren't the most comfortable, and they certainly weren't made large enough to accommodate a werewolf. Lucky for him, he needed to be up early so he could look into getting Angel's apology present before the conference started.

He popped into the bathroom to wash his face and fix his bed head, only to realize there was no way he could go out in his current clothes. They were rumpled from being slept in, his pants had several grass and dirt stains, and his shirt had some very obvious bloodstains.

He checked the time; it was just past 5am. Angel would either still be sleeping or out for a run. Deciding it was worth the risk, Caleb left a note telling Jesse where he'd gone, left the room and headed down the hallway. He paused for a minute outside the door to his room, trying to discern whether Angel was still in bed. Unfortunately, the hotel walls were so thin, he couldn't be sure whose steady breathing he was hearing. Moving quickly and quietly, he slid the key card into the door and slipped inside.

The room was dark, and Caleb immediately realized Angel was, in fact, still asleep. Slowly creeping forward, he looked for a decently clean set of clothes. He found a pair of jeans at the foot of the empty bed and managed to fish socks, underwear, and a clean shirt out of his bag without making too much noise. Slipping into the bathroom, he closed the door and changed quickly. Gathering up his dirty clothes, he returned to the main room and was looking for a good place to dump them when Angel spoke.

"Hi," she said, still lying in bed, wrapped in the blankets. She looked so damn adorable in the morning.

"Uh, hi," he replied. "I, uh, just needed a change of clothes. I–"

"It's alright," Angel told him, "don't worry about it."

"Okay," he said, finally remembering the clothes in his hand and dumping them next to his bag.

"I, um, I mean we–" he began, but she interrupted.

"We should talk about last night," she said.

"We should," Caleb agreed.

"Later, though," Angel told him. "Tonight?"

"Tonight's the big dinner. How about lunch? Meet me here?"

"Sounds good," Angel said, smiling a little. "See you then."

"I'm looking forward to it," Caleb told her. "I'll let you get back to sleep. Sorry for waking you."

Caleb left the room without waiting for a reply, knowing it was probably for the best; if he stayed much longer, he would likely crawl into bed with her, and their fight would stay unresolved. He closed the door softly, then headed down the hallway, taking the stairs down to the lobby and out the parking lot. He climbed into his car, pulled up directions on his GPS, and followed the machine's prompts until he pulled up to a nondescript looking group of businesses. Thankfully, the one he was looking for was already open. He parked on the street and headed inside the small shop. A bell tinkled overhead as he entered, and a voice from the back room called out.

"Be with you in a moment!"

After about a minute, a very large, balding man emerged from the back room.

"How can I help you?" he asked.

"You're the owner?" Caleb asked.

"Yep, that's me," he replied, coming around the corner and holding out his hand. "I'm Carl. What can I do for you today?"

CHAPTER 33

Angel tried to go back to sleep after Caleb left, but it was no use. Throwing back the covers, she climbed out of bed and pulled out her running clothes. In ten minutes flat, she was dressed and out in the parking lot, stretching and trying to figure out which direction to go. Choosing distance over difficulty, she decided to run along the road. It was a lovely morning, and after the first mile, she found herself relaxing more and thinking about her fight with Caleb less. She turned around after about half an hour, leaving herself lots of time to get showered, dressed, and fed before the conference started for the day.

As she arrived back at the hotel, Angel noticed Caleb's SUV wasn't in the parking lot. She was a bit curious about where he would have gone so early but figured she could ask him later. She headed back to the room, showered and dressed, then headed downstairs to grab breakfast. She loaded her plate up with eggs, bacon, and pancakes, grabbed a big mug of coffee, and grabbed an empty seat at Jesse's table.

"Morning," she greeted, taking a big gulp of hot coffee.

"Morning," Jesse replied. "How are you?"

"Good."

"You sure?" Jesse asked.

Angel noticed he wasn't the only one giving her a concerned look. Jonathan was sitting across from his son, watching her closely.

"I'm fine," she repeated, "really."

"Do you know where Caleb went this morning?" Jesse asked.

"Nope," Angel replied, digging into her pancakes. She got three bites into her mouth before she realized she was being watched. Jesse and Jonathan, and even Matt, were studying her intently. "What?" she asked around a mouthful of food. "Why are you looking at me like that?"

"Are you sure you're okay?" Jonathan asked in a serious tone.

"Oh, seriously!" Angel shouted, drawing attention from several wolves at nearby tables. "We had a fight. People have fights all the time," she explained, "it's not the end of the world."

"You seemed pretty mad last night," Jesse remarked.

"I was annoyed, and upset," Angel clarified. "If I'd really been mad, I would have thrown a couple spells at him and laughed."

Jesse chuckled, stopping abruptly when he realized she wasn't joking. "Oh," he said. "I see. Okay, then."

"Can I eat my breakfast now?" Angel asked.

"What? Oh, yeah, yeah, don't let us stop you," Jesse said, looking a little uncomfortable.

"Thank you," Angel replied sarcastically, turning her attention back to her food.

That morning, Angel was surprisingly paired with Matt for security detail. When she asked him about it, he just shrugged and led her down the hallway. They were assigned to sweep the interior of the hotel.

"Figured you might not want to spend too much time with Dr. Phil today," he said, gesturing to Jesse, who was heading off with his father for the first morning talk.

"Thanks," Angel told him. "So, did you learn anything useful from our fanged friends last night?"

"They were hired through an online ad," Matt explained. "Some anonymous person said he would pay them a thousand bucks each to show up at the hotel and wander around. They weren't informed it would be full of werewolves."

"Talk about 'too good to be true,'" Angel observed. "So either the threats are credible and this was someone's way of testing our defenses, or someone has a really awful sense of humor."

"I'm leaning a little more towards the former," Matt said.

"Me, too," Angel agreed.

"I've increased the number of people covering the perimeter at night," Matt told her. "Is there anything else you could do with your magic?"

Angel was surprised he was asking for her help so easily, especially about magic, but she figured it wouldn't help to point it out.

"Not really," she said, "I mean, I could set up another perimeter to give us a little more warning, but I don't imagine it would be that useful."

"You can't do anything to trap them or keep them from crossing the perimeter?"

"Not unless I'm out there all the time," Angel explained, "and it would be pretty draining. Vampires are resistant to most magic, like wolves. Aside from premixed potions, which I've already explained are highly controlled, only a few spells are truly effective against vampires. I've used a few of them once or twice, in training, but never in the field."

"Like what?"

"Witchfyre is the first one that comes to mind," Angel replied, continuing when it became clear Matt had no idea what she was talking about. "Witchfyre is magical fire witches can create and direct to do what they want. It can't be put out by water, and it can burn through anything. Unfortunately, it's very difficult to control on your own; the rare times it is used, several witches have to work together to make sure it doesn't get loose and destroy everything."

"Let's not try that one, then," Matt said. "Anything else?"

"I know a freezing spell that would probably work," she suggested, "but it's meant to be used to cool down your drink or flash freeze food, not zombies. I could maybe freeze a limb or two, but not a whole body. Besides that, the best I could do is put up magical barriers. It would hold a few zombies for a short period of time."

"You've also set up that ward," Matt noted, "so at least we'll have some sort of warning before they're on top of us."

"Yeah," Angel agreed, liking this newer, nicer side of Matt. "Way to look on the bright side!"

He just grunted and kept walking.

CHAPTER 34

Lunchtime came, and Angel was a lot more nervous than she'd expected herself to be. She hadn't seen Caleb all morning, and doubts were starting to invade her thoughts. Sure, he'd said they needed to talk, but maybe this fight had made him realize she wasn't worth his time; they were just too different to be together. Her wolf was totally unperturbed, confident Caleb wouldn't give up on them. He was an Alpha, and he should have a Mate just as strong, a Mate who could and would challenge him where no one else would. Angel tried to believe in her other half, but she still felt a little sick to her stomach as she bade farewell to Matt and headed upstairs.

She hesitated a moment at the door, then straightened her spine, slid in her key card, and entered the room. Caleb was sitting on one of the beds, reading a book. Angel took a few steps forward, letting the door close behind her, and squinted at the title; it read A Guide to Witches. It was a book intended to teach humans the basics about witches. Things like what they can and can't do with magic, the laws they have to follow, and other useful bits of information. What she couldn't figure out was why a werewolf was reading such a book.

"Oh, hey, you're back," Caleb said, finally noticing her. He slipped a receipt into the book as a makeshift bookmark, then set it on the bedside table. "How was your morning?"

"Uh, pretty good," Angel replied. "I worked with Matt; he's being a lot nicer to me now. Why are you reading that?" She gestured to the book.

"Oh, well, I saw it when I was out shopping," Caleb explained, coming to stand in front of her, "and I realized I really don't know that much about witches. I asked the lady at the bookstore what she recommended, and she sold me this. Is it any good?"

"It is," Angel told him, "but it's mostly written for humans."

"I can tell," Caleb said, "but it still seems to have a lot of good information."

"Thank you."

"For what?"

"For caring enough to try and learn more about witches," Angel replied.

Caleb grinned widely, took a step forward, and wrapped his arms around her. Angel returned the hug, enjoying the closeness.

"Of course I care," he said. He held her for a moment longer before stepping back and taking her hands in his. "I owe you an apology for last night," he said. "I stepped in when I shouldn't have; you were handling things perfectly fine on your own."

"Apology accepted," Angel told him. "And I apologize for overreacting. I know you were just doing what Alphas do, and as much as it bugs me to be protected sometimes, if I want to be with you, I'm going to have to learn to deal with it."

"And I'll have to learn to ease up on the protectiveness sometimes," Caleb admitted.

"So, we're good?" Angel asked.

"Not quite," Caleb said, holding up a hand.

"Oh?" Angel replied, getting worried.

"I got you something," Caleb told her, pulling open one of the dresser drawers and taking out a box. "I figured you weren't really a flowers kind of person, so I tried for something more your style." He held the box out to her and smiled.

"You didn't have to get me anything," Angel protested, but Caleb shook his head.

"I wanted to," he said, pushing the box towards her again, "take a look."

"Okay, okay," Angel said, taking the box. It was made of

wood and had a decent weight to it. She placed it on the bed, undid the latch, and flipped open the lid.

Caleb was on pins and needles, waiting to see how Angel would like her gift. He'd spent nearly an hour with Carl, learning more about weapons than he'd ever thought he would, but if she liked her present, it would be completely worth it. This wasn't just an apology gift; it was a way for him to show he cared about her, and he knew her well enough to get it right. He watched anxiously as Angel opened the box.

"Oh my God," she said quietly, and Caleb had a moment of panic that he'd chosen wrong. But then she let out a very uncharacteristic squeal and launched herself at him. "Thank you, thank you, thank you!"

"I take it you like them?" Caleb asked.

"I love them," Angel replied, pulling back and planting a kiss on his lips. "You're amazing, did you know that?"

"You're pretty impressive yourself," he told her. "Why don't you take a closer look?"

Angel gave him another kiss before letting him go and returning her attention to her gift. Reaching down, she gently lifted one of the throwing knives from the box. They were black - some sort of carbon fiber material that was super light and wouldn't rust - with a triangular blade, and a flat, rounded handle. Carl had assured him they were perfectly balanced, which apparently was a good thing for throwing knives. Angel was examining the blade, weighing it in her hand and checking out the leather sheaths that came with the set.

"These are incredible," she told him, replacing everything in the box. "How did you ever find such a great present?"

"Well, I figured there couldn't be too many weapons shops in town," he explained, "so I checked the phone book, found Carl's place, and asked him if there was anything you'd looked at when you were there the other day but didn't buy. He mentioned you'd checked out some of his throwing knives but hadn't bought any because you were already buying your swords."

"Thank you," Angel said, stepping forward and taking his hands in hers, "this is a wonderful surprise."

"You're welcome," Caleb told her.

She smiled at him, then gave him a mischievous look.

"How much time do you have for lunch?"

He grinned back at her.

"Long enough."

Angel stretched out across the bed, relaxed, and immensely satisfied. Caleb trailed his fingers along her side, and she turned, cuddling up to him.

"There's probably going to be no food left by the time we get downstairs, but that was totally worth it."

"Agreed." Caleb glanced at the clock and frowned.

"Come on," she said, climbing off the bed and gathering up their clothes. "We've both got work to do."

They dressed quickly, but Angel took a couple more minutes strapping on her new knives. Caleb was ready before her, and waited patiently for her by the door.

"Ready," she called out, pulling on her jacket, "let's go."

"Hold on," Caleb said, grabbing her before she reached the door and pulling her close.

"We really don't have time, Caleb," she said, but he put a finger to her lips to silence her.

"I'm not trying to get you in bed again," he said.

"Then what is it?"

"I love you."

"You–"

"I love you, Angel."

"Oh," she replied lamely.

"I know this - us - isn't going to be the easiest thing," he said, "and I don't know if it's going to be forever, but right here, right now, I love you. And I wanted you to know."

"I love you, too, Caleb," Angel said, grinning broadly.

Caleb returned her smile, then leaned down and pressed a gentle kiss to her lips. It warmed her from head to toe and made her wolf giddy.

"Come on," Caleb said, taking her hand, "let's try and find some lunch."

CHAPTER 35

The afternoon seemed to pass in a blur. Angel was paired with Jesse, and they dutifully followed Jonathan from room to room. Around 5pm, they headed to the ballroom where Matt was waiting to go over the security details for the night. Jonathan was hosting a dinner party, one of the few events of the week where every Alpha and their entourage would be in attendance. This fact was apparently causing the grumpy wolf to stress out.

"You're late," he grumbled as they arrived.

Jesse checked his watch, which read 5:15pm.

"You said five-fifteen. It's five-fifteen."

"Not according to my watch."

Angel just shrugged, then grinned when she saw Caleb across the room. He waved, and she returned the gesture.

"Right," Matt said, pulling her attention back to him. "You and Jesse are covering the back door tonight. We've also got an entrance on the right side of the room that leads into the kitchens. I'll be rotating around the room every fifteen minutes. If you see anything out of place, text me. Got it?"

Angel nodded. "Got it."

"Pretty straightforward," Jesse added.

"Good." He pointed to a table nearby that had a big tray of sandwiches on it. "I suggest you eat something now. People should start showing up in about twenty minutes."

They headed for the sandwiches, grabbing a few and sitting to eat. Angel was getting started on her second one when Jesse spoke up.

"Looks like you and Caleb made up."

"Mmmhmm."

"Good. You two are a good match."

Angel chewed thoughtfully, then swallowed. "You really think so?"

He nodded. "Definitely."

Caleb watched Angel with Jesse, only a little jealous he wouldn't be able to work with her tonight. But considering how easily distracted he was when she just walked into the room, it was probably for the best. He glanced down at the documents he was supposed to be reviewing for the night but kept finding his attention back on Angel. He found himself thinking back on the past week, and the changes in their relationship. She loved him - a revelation she'd freely provided - and the knowledge warmed him immensely. They'd had their first fight and recovered from it well, which he'd heard was a good sign. For now, things were going well, and Caleb was hopeful they'd continue that way.

Being an Alpha, he was the kind of person to evaluate and analyze situations, relationships included. As far as he and Angel were concerned, he saw two potentially major hurdles ahead of them. Firstly, he was worried when they got back to Waterloo, she might go back to trying to deny her feelings for him. Unfortunately for her, now that he knew the truth, he was unlikely to be as passive with his advances. If he needed to throw her over his shoulder and drag her off to his bedroom, then that's exactly what he'd do. And he was quite certain they'd both enjoy every minute of it.

The second hurdle he saw was the secrets Angel had mentioned earlier in the week. Obviously, it was something significant, given how much she'd resisted getting close to him. In truth, he was less concerned about what the secrets were, and how he'd be able to convince her she could trust him with them. Unfortunately, he was drawing a blank on ideas. His wolf wasn't super helpful either; wolves tended to rely on the basics when it came to wooing females. Kill something big and bad, like a buck or a bear, and prove you're strong enough to protect a female, and provide for her and her pups. Caleb didn't think Angel would be too impressed with a dead animal, no matter how big it was.

Speaking of his wolf, the beast was still being less than clear when it came to knowing whether or not Angel was their Mate. At this point, Caleb was just assuming this was another one of the challenges that went with being an Alpha. Sometimes, you had to make big decisions without all the necessary information, and good leaders had to figure out how. Fortunately, it wasn't like he had to make the decision today. He knew Angel was nowhere near ready to make that kind of commitment, and he breathed a little easier knowing he still had time to sort things out with his other half. He tore his attention away from the incredible female who'd stolen his heart and tried his best to focus on the words in front of him.

CHAPTER 36

Hunger and rage drove Alice forward, the scent of blood and fear so close, she could practically taste it. A small portion of her mind told her it was people she was smelling - living humans - but the monster she'd become only saw food. She jostled against the others surrounding her, not even caring when she found herself next to a Quiet One. The creature moved quickly but still awkwardly, its face stuck in the same blank expression as all the others. She heard screams, growls, and a blaring alarm, but nothing slowed her down. They poured into the building, the artificial lighting temporarily blinding her, but she used her other senses to find her prey. Heartbeats and footsteps ahead. The smell of perfume and sweat. She reached out, grabbing at flailing limbs, and managed to get hold of an arm. Quick as lightning, she sank her fangs into the tender flesh and drank deeply. Her prey fought back briefly, pushing at her head and desperately trying to free themselves, but it was no use. Alice drank until they stopped moving. And then she went looking for more.

CHAPTER 37

"This is intense," Angel said to Jesse shortly after the last Alpha arrived at the ballroom. She didn't bother trying to whisper; everyone still would have heard her anyway.

"What do you mean?"

"The energy in the room, with so many Alphas. It's almost like the air is thicker."

Jesse eyed her curiously. "You can feel that?"

Angel shrugged, trying to seem nonchalant, but worried she'd somehow given herself away.

"It's magic, right? I know it's not usually something that really comes up, but it's magic that makes werewolves able to change. It's magic that makes an Alpha. Why wouldn't I be able to feel it?"

"I suppose you're right," Jesse said. "I guess I never thought of it that way. And I suppose most witches never get this close to so many Alphas in once place."

"That's probably a good thing," Angel pointed out.

"How come you get along so well with wolves?"

"Well, as an agent, I figured there was a possibility I might need to interact with wolves as part of my job, so I learned what I could about them, and how to best interact with packs. But I'm guessing you're more interested in why I don't have the same prejudices most witches seem to have about wolves?"

"You are definitely in the minority when it comes to witches who treat us like actual people."

"My mother hates werewolves." Jesse gave her a stunned look, and she couldn't help laughing a little. "I know, it doesn't seem all that intuitive, but let me explain. My mom hates werewolves, and it's always something she's been pretty vocal about.

When I was younger, I just went along with it, but as I got older, I noticed her hatred really only hurt her. She let it consume such a large part of her life, and it just made her angry whenever the topic came up. I decided I didn't want to be like that."

"That actually makes a lot of sense," Jesse said. "I'm glad you made that decision."

Angel couldn't help grinning, her eyes finding Caleb despite the full room.

"Me, too."

Dinner was served - all eight courses - and the hotel staff were getting things prepped for dessert and coffee when Jonathan stood, his mere presence demanding attention. Angel was once again impressed at how easily he could manipulate his Alpha power when and how he wanted. In under a minute, the room was silent, and all eyes faced forward.

"I want to thank you all for making the time to be here this week," Jonathan began, but after the first few words, Angel tuned him out. Something at the periphery of her senses told her something was wrong. Then the first jolt of magic hit her. And then another. And another. And another, until she couldn't tell the individual jolts apart. She turned down her connection to the ward, took a deep breath, and shouted as loud as she could.

"Breach!"

Everyone jumped into motion. Jesse charged forward, forcing his way through the crowd to Jonathan. Caleb joined them, coming up behind her. Matt was already at his Alpha's side.

"North of the hotel," she said before anyone could speak. "I don't know if it's vampires or zombies, but there's a lot of them. The south still seems pretty safe, but we need to get everyone out of here now."

Matt nodded, barked a few orders to some wolves nearby, and a moment later someone pulled the fire alarm. People started to file out of the ballroom, and Angel moved to help.

"No," Matt said, touching her shoulder briefly, "you go with Jonathan. I'll make sure everyone clears out."

"Alright," Angel said, moving to join Jonathan, Jesse, and Caleb as they exited the room.

They made it down the hallway and into the lobby before the screaming started. Hotel staff ran past them, some bleeding from bite wounds, trying to escape, but the front doors were clogged with people. Angel yanked off her jacket and pulled one of her swords free from its holster.

"Side exit," Jesse shouted, leading them away from the main lobby and towards the restaurant.

They moved through the dining room and into the kitchens. No one was around; Angel assumed they'd left when they heard the fire alarm. At least until the smell of blood and death and rot hit her nose. Jesse pulled them to a stop about ten feet from the exit, taking a few tentative steps towards the door.

"You smell that?" Jesse asked.

Caleb and Jonathan nodded.

"You're sure they're coming from the north, Angel?" Caleb asked.

"Yep," Angel replied. "But there's enough of them that they could have made their way around to this door by now."

"Could be the wind is carrying their scent," Jonathan noted.

Jesse took a few more steps forward and pressed his ear against the door. Giving them a here goes nothing look, he pushed the door open a crack.

"Fuck!" he shouted, leaping back as a couple zombies pushed through the doorway.

One of them reached for Jesse, and Angel pulled a knife, flinging it across the room. It hit the zombie between the eyes, and he dropped instantly. Caleb jumped forward, grabbed one of the still standing monsters, and snapped his neck in one swift motion. Jesse went after another one, but they were still coming in through the open door. Reaching out with her magic,

Angel pulled the door shut. The others managed to dispatch the remaining zombies quickly, she retrieved her knife, and then they were on the move again.

"Now what?" Angel asked.

"We go through the restaurant," Jesse said. "There's an exit that bypasses the lobby and lets out into the parking lot. Hopefully, they haven't made it that far yet."

They made it through the restaurant, running into Matt, Serguei, and Martin.

"The front door is crazy," Matt told them, "everyone is trying to get out that way.

"We've got another way," Jonathan said, "come on."

They ran past the elevator bank and the entrance to the stairwell, down a hallway marked "Staff Only." From the smell of detergent, bleach, and fabric softener, Angel guessed the hotel laundry was nearby. They rounded a corner, Jesse in the lead, and nearly ran right into a group of zombies. The ugly creatures lurched towards them, reaching out with rotting hands.

"Ah, hell," Jesse cursed.

"Move back," Angel shouted, and Jesse and the other wolves listened. Weaving her magic quickly, she created a barrier in the hallway, stopping the zombies from moving any further.

"Nice one," Caleb told her.

"Yeah," Angel replied, "but it won't hold for long. We have to get out of here."

They made it back to the elevators, intending to try to the front doors again, but ran into more zombies. They moved quickly, taking out the ones that got close to them, trying to find a way out of the hotel. Unfortunately, another hallway revealed even more zombies, and they were forced to backtrack once again.

"Now what?" Caleb asked.

"They're blocking all the exits," Jesse said, "we can't get out. We need to find a more defensible position."

"The restaurant," Angel suggested, "there are only two

ways in, and there's lots of furniture we can use to barricade the doors."

"The restaurant it is," Jonathan said, and they moved quickly back to the restaurant.

Once they made sure it was zombie-free, they worked quickly, grabbing chairs and tables and stacking them in front of the doors. Angel erected magical barriers at each entrance, for all the good they would do against so many zombies. They'd just finished piling the last of the chairs against the front entrance when the zombies started pushing against the doors. They gathered in the center of the room, back-to-back.

"Anyone have any ideas to get us out of here in one piece?" Jonathan asked.

"No, but I'm open to suggestions," Martin replied. "I really don't feel like being zombie food tonight."

"What about witchfyre?" Matt suggested, looking to Angel.

"What the heck is that?" Jesse asked.

"Magical fire," Angel explained, "burns through anything it touches. Very powerful, very difficult to control."

"I say go for it!" Martin said as the doors out to the lobby creaked ominously with the weight of so many zombies pushing against them.

Angel shook her head. "When I say anything, I mean anything," she said. "I could lose control and easily kill one of you. Or bring the whole damn hotel down on our heads."

"Then we'll keep it as a last resort," Jonathan said. "In the meantime, we fight. Try to clear a path towards the lobby and the front door. If we can get outside, we might be able to even the odds and take them out."

The doors in front of them began to splinter and crack; zombie limbs reached into the room, pressing against Angel's barrier, then dissolving it completely. All the wolves except Caleb shifted quickly, not even bothering to get undressed first. Angel pulled out her second sword.

"You should shift, Caleb," she said.

"I'll be fine," he insisted.

Angel rolled his eyes at his stubbornness. Jesse, in wolf form, made a sound not unlike a laugh, and Caleb frowned at him. Caleb opened his mouth to say something but closed it when they heard a large bang at the door to the kitchens.

"Awesome," Angel said sarcastically. "I did mention how much I hate zombies, right?"

"Yep," Caleb said.

"If we get through this," she said to Caleb, "you owe me a real vacation. None of this werewolf conference with a risk of zombies bullshit."

"Deal," Caleb said, smiling despite the direness of the situation. "How about Hawaii?"

"Hawaii sounds perfect," Angel said, giving him a nervous smile. "Be careful, alright?"

He nodded.

"I will. You, too."

Angel nodded, turning her attention to the front door. The zombies behind it seemed to surge forward once, twice, then the door collapsed into the room. Zombies pushed forward, stumbling over the furniture that had been piled up. Some of them fell and were trampled, but more followed behind them, and in moments they'd cleared the debris and were coming for Angel and the wolves. Matt and Jesse leapt forward, grabbing rotting limbs and trying to rip apart the walking corpses piece by piece. Angel joined them, hacking at any limbs she could reach and taking off their heads when Matt got them down on the ground.

The rest of the wolves covered their backs as more zombies spilled into the room and surrounded them. Caleb, still in human form, picked up some broken chair legs and started bashing zombies in the head. The kept at it, hacking and biting and bashing at every zombie that came for them, desperately trying to move out of the restaurant, but there were just too many. Angel already had a few scrapes along her arms from where a zombie had grabbed at her; the others had similar wounds. Angel started lashing out with magic, using any spell she could think of that might help. Unfortunately, most of the spells either bounced right off the zombies or barely slowed them down. A yelp drew her attention to her left side, and Angel saw Matt on the ground, with two zombies clamped onto his back and foreleg.

"Get off, you fuckers!"

She shouted, swinging her blade quickly and beheading the first, then the second. Matt rose quickly but fell again, yelping when he tried to put weight on his injured leg. Caleb moved to stand over the injured wolf, shielding him from the zombies.

"This isn't working!" Angel screamed above the din.

Caleb swung his makeshift bludgeon and cracked open a zombie's head like a melon; brain matter sprayed across the floor. Looking around quickly, he noticed a door behind the restaurant bar. He had no idea what was behind it, but the path to it was noticeably easier, and it had to be better than this.

"Over there!" he shouted, pointing at the door.

"Right," Angel nodded. She held out her hands, and an invisible barrier seemed to push through the few zombies in their way.

Caleb bent down quickly, grabbed Matt, and threw him over his shoulder.

"Let's go!" he shouted, letting Jesse and Jonathan lead the way. Angel followed right behind him, with Martin and Serguei bringing up the rear. They made it behind the bar, and Caleb flung open the door, revealing a small stock room. "Shit!" He turned, intending to find a better option, and saw the wave of zombies coming towards them.

"Just get in!" Angel shouted, pushing them forward. The wolves followed, and she slammed the door shut, dropped her swords, and started piling boxes in front of the door. Caleb set Matt down gently, spotting a heavy looking metal shelf near the door.

"Here," he said, stepping forward and grabbing the shelf.

Angel stepped out of the way, the wolves shifted back to human, and Jesse helped him slide the shelf into place. The door creaked a little as the zombies pushed against it, but it seemed to be pretty sturdy. It wouldn't last forever, but it would give them a few minutes at least.

"Now what?" Martin asked, frantically looking around. "We're in a friggin' closet with no windows and no other door. We're sitting ducks in here!"

"Calm down," Jonathan said, imbuing his words with a subtle amount of power to calm the panicky wolf. "We'll figure something out."

"There's just too many of them," Serguei remarked, "and too few of us."

Jonathan nodded, and Caleb could practically see the wheels turning in his head, trying to figure out a plan.

"How's your leg, Matt?" Jesse asked, kneeling next to the other wolf and gesturing to the ugly bite mark on his lower leg.

"Stings like a bitch," Matt growled, "but it's healing. I should be able to walk on it shortly."

Caleb stepped over to Angel, who was wiping her swords clean with a rag she found somewhere. She had a few scrapes on her arms and legs but otherwise seemed fine.

"You okay?" he asked.

"I'm still in one piece," she replied. "As for 'okay,' ask me when there isn't a hotel full of zombies after us. You?"

"Also still in one piece," Caleb told her, grinning despite the seriousness of their situation.

"Does anyone have a cell phone?" Jesse asked. "Maybe we could call someone who got out and tell them where we are. Even the odds a little."

Caleb looked around, noting that he and Angel were the only ones still wearing clothes, and thus the only ones who might still have their phones. He patted his pockets quickly, realizing his phone had been in his jacket, which he'd discarded somewhere in the restaurant.

"I don't have mine," he replied, turning to Angel.

"Fuck, I don't either," Angel replied. "It was in my jacket."

"I think it might be time to consider our last resort," Matt said.

The door creaked loudly, and a small crack appeared in the middle. Jonathan thought for a moment before shaking his head gently.

"I'm afraid Matt might be right," he said. "What do you think Angel?"

"I can try," she replied, "but do remember I warned you about what could happen with witchfyre."

"You have," Jonathan said, "and we'll accept the potential risks. What do you need us to do?"

"Just stay back," Angel said, "and whatever you do, do not touch the witchfyre. This isn't like regular fire; it'll burn a person to ash in less than a minute. I can try a quick burst to clear out the immediate area, but I don't trust myself to maintain control for much more than that. We'll probably still have to fight our way out."

"Whatever you can do," Jonathan told her.

Angel nodded, sheathing her weapons and taking a few deep breaths.

Caleb stepped forward and put his hands on her shoulders.

"Are you gonna be alright?" he asked.

"Yeah," she said, "but it's not me I'm worried about. The witchfyre shouldn't burn me because I'm creating it, but it could easily kill any of you, werewolf healing or no."

"We understand," Caleb said, "just do your best."

"Thanks," she said, smiling nervously.

Caleb smiled back and planted a soft kiss on her lips. "You can do this," he said, and there was no doubt in his mind she could.

Angel smiled at him, took a deep breath, stepped back, and addressed everyone. "Stay behind me, as far back as you can," she instructed, "and don't move until I give the go ahead.

Got it?" Everyone nodded in the affirmative. She turned to face the door and sheathed her weapons. "Here goes nothing."

CHAPTER 38

Angel wasn't sure if it was Caleb's confidence in her abilities or the fact that she'd performed some pretty spectacular magic in the past few months, but as she faced the door and prepared to conjure witchfyre, she felt surprisingly calm. Taking another deep breath, she closed her eyes and focused on her magic. The spell to create witchfyre was relatively simple, and she completed it quickly; now all she had to do was ignite the spell, and she would have an immensely powerful weapon on her hands. She opened her eyes, pushed the shelf out of the way with her magic, and took a moment to prepare herself. Then, before she could second guess her decision to go through with this crazy plan, she pulled open the door and ignited the spell.

Zombies fell through the doorway and were engulfed in flames before they could even react. The witchfyre consumed them almost instantly, the dead flesh being extremely combustible. Within seconds, the doorway was cleared. Angel stepped forward, pushing the magical fyre forward and through the mob of zombies inside the restaurant. The fyre tore through the zombies, leaving piles of ash on the floor, burning through the remaining furniture, and scorching the walls. The magic strained to be released, almost like it was a living being, but she managed to maintain control, if just barely. In a matter of minutes, not a zombie was in sight, but Angel knew it was only a matter of time until more came after them. They needed to get out of there, and fast, but first she needed to extinguish the spell. She pulled the fyre back to her, ignoring its attempts to break free from her control. Finally, she managed to pull it back completely and extinguish the spell. She was breathing deeply, the cost of the spell weighing on her heavily.

"Is it safe?" Caleb called out. "Can we come out?"

"Yes," she replied, "it's safe."

Caleb came forward and pulled her close. "Are you alright?"

"Yep, just a little tired."

"They're all gone!" Martin exclaimed, dashing past them and through the empty restaurant.

"Wait!" Jesse called out, but it was too late; the other wolf was running quickly. He went to go after him, but Jonathan pulled him back.

"We'll find him," he told the younger wolf, "but we need to stay together." He turned to Angel. "Are you good to keep moving?"

Angel nodded, took a few deep breaths, and drew her swords.

"Yeah," she said, "let's go."

All the wolves except Caleb shifted again, and they headed in the direction of the lobby. Matt was still limping slightly, but he was able to keep up. They got through the restaurant without running into any trouble, but just as they were deciding which direction might be the safest, they heard a scream from towards the front lobby.

"That's Martin," Serguei said.

He moved to go after his friend but paused, looking to Jonathan.

"Let's go," the Master Alpha said.

They rushed down the hallway, encountering a small group of zombies as they turned a corner. Martin was on the ground, unmoving, and based on the amount of blood that covered the beige carpet, they were too late. They would have turned and headed back the other way, but there were two vampires with this group, and as soon as they caught sight of Jonathan, the zombies headed straight for them. Angel dodged the first grasping arm, turning quickly and slicing off the offending limb; the zombie's head hit the ground a moment later. Each of the wolves had a zombie to fight, and most of them were doing well, but then the vampires jumped into the fray. The first one grabbed Matt by the scruff of his neck and hurled him into the wall. The grey wolf lay still where he landed. The vampire went after Matt again, but Serguei leapt at him, drawing him away from the downed wolf. The second vampire went after Jonathan, who'd already dispatched one zombie and was helping Jesse with another. Neither wolf saw him coming.

"Jonathan!" Angel shouted, but the vampire was too fast.

He reached Jonathan before the wolf realized the danger, landing a solid kick to the Alpha's ribs. Jonathan went sprawling, and Jesse moved to try and help his father but was waylaid by a zombie. Without hesitating, Angel teleported herself just behind the vampire as he went after Jonathan again. Lifting her blade high, she used all her strength to ram the blade through the bloodsucker's back, hoping she might manage to destroy his heart.

Instead of dying, the vampire screamed in pain and turned quickly, dislodging her grip on her sword. With the blade still stuck in his back, the vampire backhanded her roughly. The blow knocked her to the ground and left her ears ringing. If she weren't a wolf, Angel suspected she would be unconscious. Trying to ignore the pain in her jaw and cheek, she pushed herself to her feet, gripped her other sword tightly, and charged the vampire again. He was standing over Jonathan - who was definitely struggling with a few broken ribs - and at that moment Angel had no doubt the Alpha was the target of this attack. Opting for a less than conventional attack this time, she struck low, hamstringing the vampire and bringing him to his knees. The blade of her other sword still protruded from his back, so she took advantage of the new angle, using her full body weight to drive it in deeper, not stopping until he made a gurgling sound and slumped to the ground.

"Angel!" Caleb cried out, coming to her side.

"I'm okay," she insisted as he gingerly touched the side of her face.

"Your face begs to differ," he remarked.

"I'll be fine," she said, pulling her sword out of the dead vampire, which was considerably easier now that he was starting to decompose. Jesse took down the vampire he was fighting and came to join them, shifting and kneeling next to his father.

"You okay, Dad?" Jesse asked.

The older wolf shifted quickly and gave his son a reassuring pat on the hand. "I'm okay," he said. "Where's Matt and Serguei?"

They all turned quickly to see Serguei in wolf form and Matt in human form, fighting the remaining vampire. Before they could move to help, the vampire threw Serguei off him and grabbed Matt by the neck, lifting him off the ground. Knowing she had seconds before the vampire snapped his neck, Angel conjured witchfyre for the second time that night and hurled it at the vampire. The spell landed on target, burning through the vampire's flesh like it was putty. Sprinting forward, Angel tried to get closer so she could extinguish the spell as soon as the vampire was dead. Unfortunately, this vampire wasn't going to go out quietly. He released Matt and thrashed wildly, trying to escape the flames, which caused the fyre to spread. Matt was on the ground at the vampire's feet, trying to catch his breath, when a flame landed on his hand. He jumped up instantly, trying to put it out, but Angel knew he wouldn't stand a chance on his own. Thinking quickly, she charged forward, struck quickly, and severed his hand at the wrist. Matt stood there in shock for a moment, staring at the bloody stump where his hand had been. Angel extinguished the witchfyre and pulled off one of her leather weapon holsters, intending to use it as a tourniquet.

"You cut off my goddamn hand!" Matt screamed at her. "What the fuck is your problem?!"

Angel tried to ignore his shouting. "Caleb, give me your shirt," she ordered. Despite his obvious shock, he complied. He pulled the shirt over his head and handed it to her silently.

"What the hell?" Jesse exclaimed.

"It was this or let the fyre kill him," Angel replied tersely, trying to get the leather strap tightened around his arm before

Matt lost too much blood. But the wolf wasn't in a cooperative mood.

"Don't you fucking touch me!" he shouted, jerking his arm away from her.

"I need to stem the bleeding," she tried to explain, but he just moved further away.

"Fuck that!"

"Matt!" Jonathan said sternly, stepping forward and taking the strap from her. "Hold still, and give me your arm."

He obeyed immediately, allowing Jonathan to apply the tourniquet.

"I'm sorry, Matt," Angel said, "it was the only thing I could think of."

Matt cast her a dirty look and turned away from her, cradling his arm close.

"Don't worry about it, Angel," Jonathan said, "it's just the shock. He'll figure it out later. Now we need to get the hell out of here."

Everyone agreed wholeheartedly. The collected Serguei, who'd only been temporarily stunned by the vampire, and once again headed for the lobby. Jesse shifted back to his wolf and took the lead, while Serguei took up the rear. Jonathan, Matt, and Caleb stayed in human form. They reached the lobby with very little resistance, which probably should have prepared them to find a huge mob of zombies and vampires blocking the front entrance. There were easily a dozen vampires, and three times as many zombies.

"Shit," Angel said.

"You can say that again," Caleb told her.

"Angel, can you teleport with another person?" Jonathan asked as every vampire and zombie turned their way.

"No idea," Angel replied, "I've never tried. Maybe."

"Take Matt."

"I can fight," Matt argued.

"Take Matt now, Angel," Jonathan repeated.

Before Matt could protest further, and before Angel

could doubt her ability to do as Jonathan asked, she grabbed the grumpy wolf and teleported outside of the hotel. They landed in the front parking lot, and Angel stumbled slightly, feeling the effects of stretching her magical limits.

"You need to get back in there," Matt told her, grabbing her shoulder with his remaining hand. "You need to help them!"

"I don't know if I can!" she replied, maybe a little more harshly than intended.

"Please," he said, softening his tone and grip, "they won't survive that without your help."

"I know," Angel said, "I know they won't, but I don't know how to help them. If I use witchfyre again, I might lose control completely and-"

"Bullshit!" Matt cursed at her. "You kicked my ass without breaking a sweat, you can take on a bunch of goddamn corpses. Or are you just as much of a pansy as I thought you were?"

Angel wasn't sure if she should hit the ornery wolf or kiss him. Sure, his methods sucked, but he accomplished his goal: he pissed her off and drew on the part of her that always liked to prove people wrong. Grinning, she slapped him on the shoulder.

"You're a real asshole, Matt," she told him. "But thanks."

Taking a deep breath and digging deep for energy she wasn't really sure she had, Angel teleported back into the hotel. She was met with a terrifying sight: four wolves fighting like hell against vampires and zombies that came at them from every side. They desperately struggled to stay together, but their attackers were too numerous and too strong. One second Jesse and Jonathan were taking down a zombie, the next Jonathan was being dragged away by a vampire. Jesse darted forward, grabbing the vamp's arm in his jaws, but a zombie came at him from behind, sinking his teeth into the wolf's back. Caleb jumped into the fray, ripping the zombie away from Jesse while Serguei took down the vampire holding Jonathan. Seeing her opening, Angel teleported into the group.

"Get down!"

She let loose a blast of energy. The wolves reacted quickly, going down on their bellies and avoiding the blast; the zombies and vampires nearest them were knocked backwards. Not wanting to give them any time to recover, Angel threw together another witchfyre spell and pushed it outward, igniting it as soon as it was clear of the wolves. The fyre burned through every enemy in a ten-foot radius, but Angel had to pull it back and extinguish it when she started to lose control. She knew she wouldn't be able to use witchfyre again safely. Looking around frantically, she spotted the front doors, only twenty feet away.

"There!" she shouted, pointing.

Jonathan looked over to where she was pointing, nodded, and charged forward. Jesse followed him, then Angel, with Caleb and Serguei right behind her. There were still too many vampires and zombies to fight, but they actually managed to make it to the door. Jonathan shifted, threw open the door, and turned to the rest of them.

"Go on, get out," he said.

Jesse shifted quickly. "What about you?"

"I'm the one they're after," Jonathan explained. "I'll lead them away."

"They'll kill you," Caleb said, coming to stand after shifting back to human, "and then they'll come after the rest of us."

"And if I come with you, they'll just follow," Jonathan replied.

Angel knew he was right; whoever was behind this attack, they wanted Jonathan dead. The attack wouldn't stop until the Master Alpha was dead, or every last vampire and zombie was.

"Caleb!" she shouted, grabbing his arm. He turned to face her, and even covered in blood and guts, he made her insides melt. "Trust me," she told him.

He looked confused for a moment, but then he nodded in understanding. He knew she had a plan, though he likely had no idea what it was. If he did, he definitely would have protested. Wrapping her magic around the four wolves, she lifted them up and hurled them out the front door, pulling the doors closed behind them. The vampires behind her screamed, furious that she'd stolen their target from them. Angel turned and was grabbed by a zombie who sank his teeth into her forearm.

"Motherfucker!" she screamed, kicking away the zombie and swinging her sword to remove his hand. But as soon as she dislodged the first one, another zombie grabbed her, sinking his teeth into her thigh. She screamed again, and deciding now was as good a time as any, she wove the spell for witchfyre, ignited it, and let it loose.

CHAPTER 39

One minute Caleb was standing at the hotel doors, debating with Jonathan about leaving him behind, the next he was hurtling through the air. He landed hard in the hotel parking lot, with Jesse, Jonathan, and Serguei right next to him. Turning quickly, he saw Angel - still inside the hotel - then the doors slammed shut.

"Angel!" he screamed, jumping to his feet and charging back towards the building.

Before he could reach it, fire exploded outward from the first floor of the hotel, knocking him on his ass. He scrambled to his feet, only to see a gaping hole where the hotel entrance used to be. The fire had spread from the main floor and was climbing steadily up the outside of the building.

"Angel!" he called out, straining to catch a glimpse of her somewhere in the wreckage. Jesse joined him, searching through the debris while trying to avoid the fire. "Do you see anything?" he asked the other wolf, pulling the remains of a door aside and finding nothing.

"No, nothing," Jesse replied. "Wait - over there!"

He pointed to an area just to the left of where the hotel entrance had been. Angel was lying face first on the ground, unmoving. Caleb dashed over and kneeled down next to her, praying she was still alive. She was covered in blood and dirt and ash, her clothes were torn, her swords were nowhere to be seen, and she wasn't moving. Ever so gently, Caleb rolled her to her back. Her eyes were closed, but he couldn't see any serious injuries. Reaching out his hand, he pressed two fingers against her neck, hoping and praying he'd find a pulse. At first he felt nothing, and his heart sank. But then, ever so softly, there it was. A steady pulse, just underneath his fingertips. She was alive.

"Is she?" Jesse asked.

"She's still alive," Caleb said, giving her a quick once over.

She had a bunch of superficial scratches, several bite marks along her arms, and her face was swollen from where that vampire had struck her. These kinds of injuries would be nothing for a wolf, but Angel was a witch, and Caleb was worried. He picked her up gently, heading away from the hotel.

"Over here!" Jonathan called them over to where he'd recovered one of the pack vehicles. Caleb set Angel down gently in the back seat, then pulled on a pair of sweatpants Matt handed him.

"Is she OK?" Matt asked.

"I think she needs a doctor," Caleb replied.

"There's a witch hospital in the south end of town," Jesse told him.

"Take the car," Jonathan said, "and take Matt with you. Jesse and I will stay here and do damage control. We'll meet up with you later."

"Thank you," Caleb told him, reaching out to shake his hand.

"I'm the one who should be thanking you," Jonathan said, "and we should all be thanking Angel. Get her whatever help she needs."

"I will. Good luck."

Jonathan and Jesse headed across the parking lot to join the hotel staff and guests who'd managed to escape the attack. Emergency vehicles were everywhere; ambulance, fire, police. Caleb grabbed a blanket from the back of the car and wrapped it around Angel. He attempted to buckle her in, but it was difficult with her lying across the back seat.

"I'll sit in the back and hold on to her," Matt offered.

"Are you sure?" Caleb asked. He wasn't entirely sure he could trust the other wolf, given how upset he'd been with Angel about his hand.

"It's not like I should be the one driving," Matt joked,

holding up the damaged limb. When Caleb didn't respond, his face became serious. "I overreacted back there," he admitted, "she saved my life, and I owe her. Let me help."

"Alright," Caleb said, moving aside and letting him climb into the back seat. Once Matt was settled, with Angel held securely in his good arm, Caleb climbed into the driver's seat.

"You ever been to a witch hospital?" Matt asked when they were about halfway through the city.

"Nope," Caleb replied.

"What do you figure it's like?"

"No idea, but when Angel was helping us with the black witch a few months back, she had these potions she took that healed her almost instantly. It would make sense, at least to me, to have that kind of thing at a hospital."

"Witches don't always make sense," Matt remarked, and Caleb couldn't help laughing a little at the very accurate observation. In the rearview mirror, he saw Matt open his mouth, pause, then close it again.

"What's up, Matt?"

"I, uh, it's just that..."

"Spit it out, Matt."

"Earlier," he said, "when Angel got me out of the hotel, she didn't seem right."

"What do you mean, 'didn't seem right?'" Caleb repeated.

"She was tired," Matt explained, "but not physically. I think she was using too much magic. Can a witch use too much magic? Is that even possible? And what happens to them if they do?"

"I don't know," Caleb replied, "but I'm sure she'll be okay."

That's what he kept telling himself - that she was going to be okay - mostly because he wasn't sure if he could deal with the alternative. He stepped on the gas, navigating around slower moving vehicles, and spotted the exit for the hospital just up ahead. A few minutes later, they pulled up in front of an average looking hospital. He would have thought it was a normal, human hospital, except for the telltale tingle of magic he felt as soon as they pulled into the parking lot. He parked in the red zone, cut the engine, and climbed out, dashing to the side door to take Angel from Matt.

"I'll park the car and meet you inside," Matt offered.

Caleb nodded and jogged up to the main doors of the hospital, which opened automatically at his approach. He found himself inside your typical hospital lobby: rows of chairs set up all around, and a desk immediately ahead of him. This time of night, no one was in the waiting room. A young man sitting at the desk looked up as he entered, a look of confusion crossing his face.

"This is a witch hospital," he said, "are you sure you're in the right place?"

"She's a witch," Caleb answered, stepping forward and resisting the urge to smack him for asking such a dumb question. "Help her."

The witch came out from behind the desk and took his first good luck at Angel. His eyes widened at the bite marks on her arms.

"What the hell happened to her?"

"Zombies," Caleb replied curtly. "Now get a damn doctor."

The man noticeably paled at the mention of zombies but went back behind the desk and picked up the phone. He dialed a number and quickly rattled off instructions to someone on the other end. As he was speaking, Matt joined Caleb in the lobby. A minute later, a set of double doors to the right of the desk opened, and a doctor marched through, following by a nurse pushing a gurney. The doctor didn't skip a beat at the two werewolves standing in the lobby of a witch hospital; he just got straight to business.

"Set her down here," he instructed, motioning to the gurney. Caleb set her down gently and stepped back, letting the doctor examine her. "What happened?" he asked, checking her pupils and examining the bite marks closely.

"Zombie attack," Caleb told him, "and vampires. She

helped us fight them off."

"You were at the werewolf conference?"

"Yes."

"What on Earth was she doing there?"

"It's a long story," Matt told him.

"Alright," the doctor said, turning towards the nurse. "Let's get her into a room and see what we can do for her." Caleb started to follow, but the doctor held out his hand, stopping him. "Wait out here, please. We'll let you know when you can see her."

Caleb watched as they wheeled Angel down the hallway and back through the double doors. He desperately wanted to go with her, but he knew he would only get in the way. So instead, he dropped into one of the waiting room chairs and waited.

CHAPTER 40

Jonathan stood and surveyed the chaos around him. The hotel was no longer on fire, but smoke billowed lazily from the wreckage. One side of the building had collapsed completely, while the other side was little more than a burnt out shell. Multiple ambulances were parked along the road, headlights left running to illuminate the parking lot. Several of them had already left, sirens blaring, carrying those with the worst injuries to the hospital nearby. The remaining paramedics had set up a triage area, handling minor bumps and scrapes. A few of the wolves attending the conference had first aid training and worked their way through the injured, helping where they could. Jonathan walked among them, lending a hand to one human paramedic who was having a difficult time convincing a wolf to let him dress the large bite wound on his arm.

"Hold still," he told the agitated man. Jonathan couldn't recall his name, but his eyes were bright, and his wolf was close. He laid his hand on the man's shoulder and pushed the wolf back, urging the beast to be calm.

"Thank you, Alpha," the male said.

Jonathan nodded and left so the paramedic could finish the job. He looked around and noticed a group of wolves standing nearby. None of them seemed injured, but they stared at the remains of the hotel, likely in shock.

"Are any of you injured?" Jonathan asked, using a bit of his Alpha voice to pull their attention away from the wreckage.

"No, Alpha," one of them replied. "We're fine."

"Good," he said, "I want you to split into groups of three and search the grounds. See if you can find anyone who needs help."

"What if we run into more of them?" a young wolf with blond hair asked, fear plain on his young face.

"Kill them," Jonathan said. "Call for help if you need to, but we can't let these monsters run free. If they get into the city, they could do a lot of damage."

The young wolf still looked frightened, but he nodded. "Yes, Alpha," he said.

The group split up and headed towards the hotel, some of them stripping quickly and shifting to their wolves. Jonathan watched them go for a moment, hoping they wouldn't run into any trouble. He was pretty sure most of the zombies had been killed in the fire, but he didn't want to take any chances.

"Dad," Jesse called out. Jonathan turned and watched as he approached. His son wore only a pair of sweatpants, much like his own, and he was covered in dirt, blood, and goodness knew what else. But he was alive.

"What is it?" he asked.

"They've set up an area for the, uh, for the dead," Jesse told him, pointing towards the far side of the parking lot.

"Show me."

Jesse led the way, taking him past the emergency vehicles to a spot where passers-by couldn't easily see. A dozen still forms lay on the grass, covered in tarps and blankets and even jackets in an attempt to provide dignity to those who hadn't survived. Jonathan visited each person, kneeling a moment and offering a few words. The dead were mostly wolves, but a few of the human hotel staff had been caught by the zombies before they could escape.

"The fire crew said they want to start recovery in the hotel as soon as the sun comes up," Jesse told him. "They're hoping the structure will hold now that the fire's out."

"I want the names of everyone who did make it," Jonathan said. "And I want to know who's missing. Wolf or otherwise."

"Got it," Jesse said, and he was off at a brisk jog.

Jonathan stayed for a few minutes, watching over the dead. He'd known this might happen, he'd weighed the risks, and he'd decided to go forward with the conference. It was one thing to imagine the consequences; it was another thing entirely to have them laid out at your feet. He knew this was only the beginning, that it wouldn't be the only fight, the only casualties. War was here, whether they wanted it or not.

CHAPTER 41

Angel woke with a raging headache, overwhelmed by the smell of antiseptic and ash. Blinking her eyes open, she tried to figure out where she was. She was lying in a bed, wearing a white gown. The room was small, painted white, with a couple machines against one wall and a shelf against the other, filled with an assortment of bottles and vials. The steady hum of magic surrounded her, and she realized she was in a witch hospital.

Sitting up slowly, things started coming back to her. The zombies, vampires, witchfyre, Martin, and Matt. Her whole body ached, but it didn't seem like anything was broken. A couple of her ribs were tender, but probably not much more than mild bruising. Lifting a hand to her head, she realized it was wrapped in gauze. At least that explained the headache. While she was still getting her bearings, a nurse entered the room, smiling when she saw Angel was awake.

"Hello, there," she said, "it's good to see you awake. How are you feeling?"

"Sore," Angel said, "and my head aches pretty badly."

"That's to be expected," the nurse said, picking up the chart at the end of the bed and flipping through it quickly. "Looks like you had a moderate concussion. We would have given you a healing potion, but your injuries weren't life-threatening, and the doctor was worried it would drain you further. We did, however, use an ointment to heal the bite wounds on your arms."

"Thanks," Angel said. "Any chance I can get something for the pain?"

"Of course," the nurse replied, pulling a small vial from

her pocket, "I've got something ready for you right here. If you need any more, just let me know."

Angel took the vial and downed it in one gulp; the pain lessened almost immediately.

"Do you think you're up for some visitors?" the nurse asked. "You've got quite a few, uh, friends, camped out in the waiting room."

"Sure," Angel replied, silently enjoying how uncomfortable the middle-aged witch seemed about having a bunch of werewolves in her hospital. "Sounds good."

"I'll send them in, but feel free to page the nurses station if you need anything."

The nurse left the room, and a minute later the door opened again. Caleb entered first, followed by Jonathan, Jesse, and, surprisingly, Matt. Words couldn't describe her relief at seeing them all in one piece.

"Hey, there," Caleb said softly. "How are you feeling?"

"Sore," Angel repeated, "but otherwise okay. What about you guys?"

"We're fine," Jesse told her. "A bit of sleep and some food, and we're nearly good as new."

"How long was I out?"

"Most of the day," Caleb said, "it's three in the afternoon on Friday."

"The zombies, and the vampires?" Angel asked.

"Destroyed in the fire," Jonathan told her. "Or the subsequent building collapse."

"Thank God," Angel said, leaning back against her pillows. Caleb grabbed a chair and set it next to the bed, sitting and taking her hand in his. "Thank you," she told him.

"For what?"

"Trusting me."

Caleb grinned at her.

"See," he said, "I can learn. But please, don't ever do something like that again. You scared the crap out of me."

Angel gave him a half-smile. "I can't make any promises,

but I'll try." Turning to Jonathan, she asked the question for which she feared the answer. "How many people were killed?"

"Seventeen confirmed so far, but there's still a number of people missing," Jonathan replied. "There were a lot more injuries, but thanks to your ward, most people got out of the hotel before the zombies got inside."

"The zombies didn't follow anyone outside?"

"It seems not."

"So they really were after you, then," Angel observed.

"Makes sense," Jonathan said. "But that's not something you need to worry about right now. Right now, you need to rest and get better."

"We're going to go grab something to eat," Jesse said. "What do you feel like?"

"Pizza," Angel answered quickly, knowing a good meal would go a long way to making her feel better.

"Pizza it is," Jesse announced. "We'll be back in about an hour."

She and Caleb were left alone in the small room, and Angel looked over to see him watching her closely.

"You're sure you're okay?" he asked, examining her closely.

"Yes," Angel said.

"Good," Caleb said, smiling at her.

They talked for a while, pausing for a few minutes when the doctor stopped by to check in on her. He was pleased with her progress and told her she should be able to leave the next day. Angel smiled, nodded, and thanked the doctor, knowing she would be mostly healed by then, but the rest would be good for her regardless. Jesse and Jonathan returned shortly after the doctor left, carrying several boxes of delicious smelling pizza.

"Gimme," Angel said, reaching out for one of the boxes, her stomach suddenly making itself heard. "I'm starving."

"Clearly," Caleb said, laughing at her. Angel just stuck her tongue out at him and took a big bite of pepperoni pizza.

It wasn't too much longer before the pizza was gone, and they were all sitting around the room, telling battle stories. Caleb and Angel shared their story about taking out the black witch Jones. Jesse told them about the time he'd been mistaken for a regular wolf by an elderly farmer with poor eyesight and a shotgun. Ten o'clock rolled around, and a new nurse poked her head inside the room, informing them visiting hours were over.

"I can have someone stay with me, right?" Angel asked.

"Yes," the nurse replied, "but only one."

"We'll see you in the morning," Jonathan said, herding the others out the door. "Sleep well."

"Goodnight," Angel said, yawning suddenly.

"You're tired," Caleb observed, coming forward and pulling up the scratchy hospital blanket. "You should get some rest."

"I slept most of the day away," she replied, her eyes feeling heavy as she struggled to stay awake.

"Sleep," Caleb told her, pressing a gentle kiss to her forehead. "I'll be here when you wake up."

"Promise?"

"Promise."

CHAPTER 42

Caleb was tired, but he couldn't seem to fall asleep. It could be the uncomfortable chair, or the constant magical buzz that tickled his senses, or it could be the little witch that slept in the bed across the room. In such a short amount of time, she'd come to mean so much to him, and last night he'd almost lost her.

The Alpha in him wanted to wrap her up and keep her safe from harm, but he knew she would never stand for that kind of treatment. He also knew one of the reasons he loved her so much was her ability to hold her own in any kind of fight. She wasn't reckless, or fearless, and she never went looking for trouble, but when it came right down to it, she wasn't one to back down easily. And yet, for all her strength, there was a softness to her he'd been lucky enough to experience. She'd opened up to him, maybe not completely, but enough for him to see the sweet, kind, loving woman who hid behind her tough outer layer.

It was then, sitting in a tiny little room, inside a witch hospital, that any questions about whether or not Angel was his Mate were answered. She belonged with him, just as much as he belonged with her, and there was no way in hell he was going to let her go again.

CHAPTER 43

Angel woke early Saturday morning feeling a lot better than she had the night before. Her body ached a lot less, and she wasn't feeling magically drained anymore. Sitting up and stretching, she saw by the clock on the wall it was just past 9am. Across from her, Caleb was sprawled out, rather uncomfortably, in a chair definitely too small for him. She almost wished she had a camera so she could take a picture. She climbed out of bed and went to use the bathroom; by the time she was finished, Caleb was awake.

"Good morning," she said.

"Good morning," he replied, standing and stretching. "How are you feeling?"

"Probably a lot better than you," she told him. "That chair was definitely not built for werewolves."

"It's not the end of the world," Caleb told her, taking a few steps and pulling her into his arms. "Besides, it was only for one night. We've got a hotel room in the city for tonight, and then tomorrow we can head home."

"Sounds like a plan," Angel said. "Though, I'm not entirely sure what I'm going to wear in the meantime. All my clothes were in the hotel, and I don't fancy trying to dig them out of the rubble."

"Don't worry about it," Caleb said, "Jonathan said they would pick up some things for you on their way over this morning."

"Great."

Angel grinned up at him and wrapped her arms around his waist; he squeezed her tightly for a moment before taking a step back. He leaned down and kissed her deeply, and the next moment he had lifted her up, carried her across the room, and sat her down on the bed. His hands skimmed up her thighs, underneath the flimsy hospital gown, and reached higher. As much as she was enjoying the attention, she forced herself to pull back and grab his hands in hers.

“I really like where you’re going with this,” she told him, “but it’s gonna have to wait until we’re not in the middle of a hospital where someone can barge in at any moment.”

“Good morning, campers!” Jesse exclaimed as he flung open the door and stepped into the room. Caleb pulled her gown back down and took a step back.

“Speak of the devil,” Angel muttered. Caleb laughed out loud.

“What was that?” Jesse asked as Jonathan stepped into the room, carrying a plastic shopping bag.

“Nothing,” Angel told him, “don’t worry about it.”

“How are you feeling?” Jonathan asked.

“Great,” Angel replied, “ready to get out of here.”

“I spoke to one of the nurses down the hall, and she said they’ll be by with release papers for you shortly,” Jonathan told her. “I also picked up some clothes for you. I hope they fit; we had to guess your sizes.”

“I’m sure they’ll be just fine,” Angel said.

“Caleb,” Jonathan began, turning to the other wolf. “Why don’t you and Jesse grab some breakfast from the cafeteria? I’d like the chance to speak with Angel alone.”

“Alright,” Caleb said, leaning down and pressing a kiss to her forehead. “Play nice, Angel. He is the ranking werewolf on this continent.”

Angel snorted. “I fought zombies for him, he can deal with my attitude.”

“Good luck,” Caleb told Jonathan as he and Jesse left the room.

Jonathan passed her the bag of clothes, and she slipped into the bathroom to change. The bag had a pair of sweatpants, T-shirt, plain cotton panties, and a bra that actually fit pretty decently. It also had some socks and tennis shoes that were a little too large, but they would do for now. She exited the bathroom to find Jonathan standing by the window.

"Thanks for the clothes," she told him, "pretty good guess with the sizes."

"It's the least I could do," he said.

"So what did you want to talk to me about?"

"I don't think the attack on the conference is the end," he said, getting straight to the point. "Whoever organized that attack was targeting me, and since they didn't manage to kill me, I don't doubt they'll try again."

"Why would they want to kill you anyway?" Angel asked, moving to sit at the foot of the bed. "I mean, yeah, you're the Master Alpha and all, but wouldn't someone else step in if you were to die?"

"Yes," Jonathan replied, "if I were to die, someone, most likely Jesse, would step in and try to take my place. But unfortunately, when a Master Alpha dies, a lot of challengers come forward to try and take on the position themselves. If I were to die, it would be months before all the challenges were properly dealt with, and in the meantime, the werewolves would be without any kind of clear leadership."

"Making them vulnerable to any potential attacks," Angel concluded. "So whoever organized this attack is trying to take down the wolves?"

"That seems to be the most obvious explanation," Jonathan told her, "but what I would like to know is who, and apart from the obvious, why."

"And you want me to help."

"I do. You've proven yourself more than capable of dealing with wolves, and I'm not too proud to admit we never would have made it out of that hotel without your help. I foresee a lot of battles in the near future, and with you on our side, I imagine we'd suffer far fewer casualties. What do you think? Will you help us?"

CHAPTER 44

Caleb was pretty sure he knew what Jonathan wanted to talk to Angel about; they all knew the attack on the hotel wasn't going to be a one-time thing. Getting Angel to help them in the coming fight was a good idea, and he was pretty sure she wouldn't need much convincing. He wasn't exactly thrilled with the idea, but he knew he would have to come to terms with it quickly, or risk spending more nights on the couch. He and Jesse grabbed a couple breakfast sandwiches from the cafeteria and were headed back to Angel's room when he heard one of the most terrifying sounds he'd ever heard.

"Where the hell is my daughter!?"

Turning quickly, he saw who he assumed was Angel's mother storming down the hallway. Though he'd never met the woman, he could see Angel favored her very strongly, with only several small features differing between them. Angel's eyes were a little different, and she was a bit taller than her mother. They did seem to share the same strength and determination, though, as the elder Myers was heading directly for him, and she was very angry. If it were physically possible, she would have had steam coming from her ears. She stopped just in front of him, somehow managing to make herself seem much taller than she actually was.

"I asked you a question! Where is she?"

"Just down the hall, room one twenty-five," he replied meekly, not wanting to upset her further.

She had every right to be angry; she'd been lied to, and her only daughter had been injured in what was supposed to be a simple security job. Elizabeth Myers stormed past him. Caleb attempted to follow, intending to provide Angel with a little moral support, but the older witch whirled on him, jabbing her finger into his chest.

"You will stay here, away from my daughter," she demanded.

He complied, but only because this was neither the time nor the place to press the issue. Elizabeth turned sharply and continued down the hallway towards Angel's room.

"Who the hell was that?" Jesse asked.

"Angel's mother," Caleb replied.

"Oh. Shit."

CHAPTER 45

Angel knew, despite her desire never to see another vampire or zombie ever again, she had to help Jonathan. Even if her involvement made no difference whatsoever, there was no way she could let them face this threat alone. If the vampires were able to take down the wolves, what would stop them from going after the witches next? She opened her mouth to say "Yes," but before she had a chance to speak, her mother barged into the room. And boy, was she pissed. Angel was pretty sure she was about to get quite the earful. As expected, Elizabeth Myers took a deep breath, opened her mouth, and paled the instant she caught sight of Jonathan. Even more surprising was the fact that she just stood there, gaping like a fish out of water, for a good minute until Angel recovered enough to speak up.

"Mom," she began, "I already know what you're going to say, and you're right, I shouldn't have lied to you."

"Mom?" Jonathan repeated, repeatedly looking between the two of them. "Angel is your daughter?"

"Mind your own damn business!" Elizabeth replied rudely.

"Uh, Jonathan, this is my mother, Elizabeth. Mom, this is Jonathan, the Master Alpha of North America."

"We already know each other," Jonathan replied softly.

"What?! What do you mean, you already know each other? Mom?" Angel looked between Elizabeth and Jonathan, waiting for one of them to answer.

"We dated for a while when we were younger," Jonathan explained.

"You 'dated for a while?'" Angel exclaimed, shocked at the revelation about her mother's past.

"At least until he dumped me for some woman he just met!" her mother spat.

"I already explained this to you, Liz," Jonathan said, "she was my Mate."

"And I still think it's a load of crap. And don't call me that!"

"Okay," Angel said, standing and moving to get between Jonathan and her mother. "Why doesn't everyone just calm down."

"I'll calm down as soon as he leaves," her mother replied, crossing her arms across her chest.

"And I'll leave as soon as you answer one question," Jonathan said, taking an equally defiant stance.

"Uh, sure," Angel replied, not entirely sure where this was going but immensely interested after seeing her mother's reaction to him.

"How old are you, Angel?"

Elizabeth visibly stiffened, though Angel had no idea why.

"Uh, twenty-eight in March. Why?"

A variety of emotions crossed Jonathan's face: anger, sadness, and even a little joy, but after a moment he pulled himself together, and his face became like a mask, giving nothing away. He turned to her mother, his voice tight.

"Why didn't you tell me, Liz?"

Angel was momentarily confused. She looked to her mother, saw the guilt plastered on her face, and suddenly everything fell into place. Jonathan wasn't just some guy her mother had dated.

"You lied to me," she said to her mother.

"I didn't–" Elizabeth began, but Angel cut her off.

"You lied to me! You told me you didn't know who my father was! You told me you were attacked!"

"I did it to protect you."

"Protect me from what? My own father?"

"She's my daughter," Jonathan interjected. "I would have

welcomed her into my pack, into my family."

"He left me," Elizabeth explained, ignoring Jonathan completely. "He didn't want anything to do with me. How was I supposed to know how he would react to you?"

"You tell him!" Angel exclaimed. "Or you wait until I'm old enough and tell me, and let me make the decision. Anything but lie to everyone!"

"Please, Angel," her mother implored, reaching out to take her hand.

"Don't touch me!" Angel snapped, stepping out of her reach.

"Angel–"

"No, Mom. Just, no." Angel held up her hands, warding away her mother.

She turned and paced the small room for a few moments, trying to wrap her head around this whole mess. Her mother had lied to her. Jonathan was her father. She had a father. Hell, she had a whole family! A sudden realization slammed into her, freezing any potential excitement she had about her new family situation. If it came out she was Jonathan's daughter, everything would change. People would treat her differently, she would probably lose her job, and most importantly, it would be a lot harder to keep her hybrid nature a secret. And all the while, vampires and zombies would need to be hunted down and dealt with before they hurt innocent people. It was all just too much. She needed time to figure things out; time to process everything. She need time alone, and she wasn't going to get it here.

"Get out," she said numbly, looking first to her mother, then Jonathan. "Please, just leave. I need to be alone."

"Alright," Jonathan said. "But if you need anything, I'm here."

"Thank you," Angel told him. He nodded, gave her mother one last indecipherable look, and left the room.

"Angel," her mother practically whispered. "I did it to protect you. Please try to understand."

"Please leave," Angel told her, determined not to get pulled into an argument. Right now, there was nothing her mother could say to make things better. In time, she might be able to see things her way, but not now; everything was just too raw.

Elizabeth opened her mouth, paused, and closed it slowly. She nodded, then turned on her heel and left the room.

Caleb could hear well enough to know there was an argument going on in Angel's hospital room, but that was pretty much expected. He knew what her mother thought of werewolves, and considering Angel had lied to her about what she was doing and who she was doing it with, Elizabeth probably had a good reason to be upset.

"Whoa," Jesse remarked. "Is Angel's mom always that intense?"

"I can't really say," Caleb replied, "I haven't met her before, mostly just overheard phone conversations. When it comes to wolves, though, she's not particularly fond of our species as a whole."

"That sucks, man," Jesse told him. "I mean, what with you and Angel being together. I can't imagine her mother is going to make that easy."

Caleb shrugged. "While I'd prefer it if her mother was at least accepting of us being together, it's what Angel thinks of me that counts."

"Good point."

The shouting died down a little, and after a few minutes Jonathan left the room. He looked mad, which wasn't really a surprise; Elizabeth didn't save her manners for wolves.

"I probably should have warned you about Angel's mother," Caleb said. "I never really thought it would be an issue. Sorry."

"You don't have to apologize," Jonathan told him. "I–"

"You! Where do you think you're going?" Ms. Myers strode

purposefully down the hall, pinning Jonathan with her gaze. "You knowingly put my daughter in harm's way, in the way of zombies and vampires! Did you really think I was just going to let that go?"

Jonathan took a deep breath before answering. "Angel is a grown woman," he explained, "and as far I can tell, she is perfectly capable of making these decisions for herself. I informed her of the risks - all of them - and she decided to take the job."

Jesse scurried off, mumbling something about fresh air, and Caleb decided it might be in his best interest to escape before Elizabeth went after him as well. He snuck past the witch and down the hall to Angel's room, managing to slip inside without her mother noticing.

"Well, that could have gone better," he said, realizing as the words left his mouth that he was in an empty room. Assuming she was in the bathroom, he went and knocked on the door. "Angel? Are you in there?"

When she didn't respond, he pressed his ear to the door and heard nothing. He pulled open the door, finding the bathroom empty as well. He checked the room again, in case he'd missed something, but didn't find any sign of her. He was about to leave and check with the nurse's station when his newly replaced phone rang. Jesse's name flashed across the screen.

"Hello?" Caleb answered, a little confused as to why Jesse was calling.

"Do you know why Angel is outside in the parking lot?"

"Probably trying to escape her mother," Caleb replied, a little relieved. "Tell her I'll be out in a minute."

"Uh, I would," Jesse said, "but she's leaving."

"What do you mean, leaving?"

"I mean, she's walking out of the parking lot and down the street," Jesse explained. "I waved to her and called her name, but she just looked over at me and kept walking."

"Follow her."

"I am, I am," Jesse said, and Caleb heard heavy footfalls through the phone. "Oh, shit."

"What?"

"She's gone."

"Gone?"

"Yeah, she just transported, or teleported, or whatever it is she does. She's gone. I don't see her anywhere."

"Keep looking," Caleb told him, ending the call and jamming his phone into his pocket. He left the room, only to see Jonathan and Elizabeth still fighting in the hallway. "Angel's gone," he shouted, silencing them both instantly.

"What do you mean, gone?" Elizabeth asked.

"I mean, she left her room, walked through the parking lot, and teleported somewhere," Caleb explained.

"You're sure?" Jonathan asked.

"Her room is empty, and Jesse saw her leaving the parking lot," Caleb replied.

"This is just some kind of trick!" Ms. Myers insisted, walking quickly down the hallway and going back into the hospital room. She exited a moment later, marching down the hallway. "This is all your fault," she spat at Jonathan as she passed him and continued towards the lobby and out the front doors. Jesse strode in a moment later, jogging up to them, his phone still in his hand.

"Anything?" Caleb asked hopefully.

"Nothing," Jesse replied. "She's gone."

CHAPTER 46

Jonathan sighed deeply, shoved away the box of cold pizza, leaned back in his chair, and propped his feet up on the desk. It had been a long week, capped off by a very long day. First he finds out Angel is his daughter, and then she goes and disappears. He couldn't really blame her; finding out your mother has lied to you all your life isn't exactly easy to deal with. Heck, finding out you have an adult daughter isn't exactly easy to deal with either.

Jonathan had always wanted a daughter. He and Melanie had three wonderful sons, and he wouldn't trade them for anything, but he'd always like the idea of having a little girl he could spoil and protect. But Angel wasn't a little girl anymore; he'd missed out on most of her life, and he couldn't help wondering if she would want anything to do with him now. Elizabeth might have doubted how her daughter would be treated, but if Angel would have them, she'd be welcomed into his family quite happily.

After she'd disappeared from the hospital, Caleb had been worried for her health and insisted on searching for her. Jonathan could have explained the reason for her disappearance, but he hadn't wanted to betray Angel's confidence. So, they'd spent the rest of the morning searching the area surrounding the hospital. When it became clear she wasn't there, they'd expanded their search, checking hotels, restaurants, and every witch-related store they could find in town. Still, they'd found no sign of her. Given she could teleport at will, Jonathan had a distinct feeling Angel wouldn't be found unless and until she wanted to be found. So they'd admitted defeat, grabbed some pizza, and headed back to the hotel, and now Jonathan was debating whether he should get some sleep or stay up and deal with the mountain of paperwork he had to deal with after the attack on the conference. Deciding he probably wouldn't get much sleep anyway, he pulled his feet off the desk, righted his chair, and started working through the first stack of papers. After a few minutes, a strange tingling sensation made him pause. Setting down his pen, he looked up, searching the room for the source of his discomfort.

"Angel?" he called out uncertainly. A moment later, she stepped around the corner.

"Hi," she replied.

"Are you okay?" Jonathan asked.

She took a few steps into the room and shrugged.

"No idea," she said. "I'm sorry about my mother."

"You don't have to apologize for her, Angel," Jonathan said, "none of this is your fault."

"Yeah, but it's not like you're gonna get an apology from her," she replied. "You think crazy is genetic?"

"Your mother isn't crazy," he assured her, "just a little intense."

Angel laughed.

"Up until he got engaged, my mother thought I should try and get back together with a witch I knocked unconscious."

"Caleb told me about that," Jonathan replied, laughing as well. "From what he told me, you saved him from a well-deserved maiming."

Angel clasped her hands in front of her and shifted nervously. "There's something else you should know about me."

"What is it?"

She took a deep breath and exhaled loudly, then stepped forward, pulling a small silver ring off her pinky finger. She set it on the desk. Jonathan picked it up and felt the telltale tingle of magic.

"What is this?"

"A spell to hide my scent."

Jonathan had a very good idea of what she wanted him

to know, but he needed to be certain. He stood and came around the desk, stopping just a foot away from her. He inhaled deeply, and her scent immediately confirmed his suspicions.

"You're a hybrid."

She nodded, a little fear in her eyes.

He hesitated only a moment before reaching out and enveloping her in a hug. She tensed up at first but relaxed quickly, wrapping her arms around his back.

"Well, that's certainly going to make things interesting."

"I don't want to put you or your family at risk," she began, but he shushed her and stepped back.

"Our family," he corrected. "And that's not something you need to worry about. Whatever you want to do - keep your true nature a secret or let it out - we'll support you."

"But–"

"No buts. That's what family is for."

"Really?"

"Really."

Jonathan could tell his words affected her deeply; she'd obviously been afraid he wouldn't want anything to do with her. Tears glistened in her eyes for a moment, then she pulled herself together.

"Thank you," she told him, "that really means a lot. I'd like to meet your - our - family, but not yet. I still need some time to work stuff out."

"Of course, I understand. What about Caleb?"

"What about him?"

"He's your Mate," Jonathan stated.

"Yeah," Angel replied sadly, "but he doesn't know. The spell that hides my real scent also keeps him from realizing I'm his Mate."

"He loves you," Jonathan told her. "He may be a little confused about your scent, but he can't hide the way he feels."

"I know," she said, "but what will he think when he finds out the truth? When he finds out I lied to him? I could put him and his pack in danger, just for being what I am."

"Caleb will understand why you didn't tell him, and from what I've heard, his family already likes you, and his pack owes you their lives. I won't lie and say things will be easy if the world finds out you're a hybrid, but I truly believe you, and the people who care about you, will be more than strong enough to handle it."

Angel gave him a soft smile. "Thank you," she said. "I think a part of me knows that, but it's still scary. My whole life will change. I'd definitely lose my job, which doesn't really seem like a big deal in the grand scheme of things, but I like what I do, I like helping people. I don't know what I'd do without that."

"You could always work for me as an Enforcer," Jonathan offered.

"You don't think the other Alphas would have a problem with a hybrid enforcer?"

"I'm sure you'd be able to handle any issues that come up," Jonathan told her, grinning. "And if they really have a problem, they can bring it up with me."

Angel smiled at him.

"Thanks," she said.

"No problem. Are you going to see Caleb? He's worried about you."

"I know he is, but I need some space right now."

"Then at least call him, so he doesn't worry so much."

"I will," Angel told him. "I should probably get going." She grabbed the ring from the desk and slid it back on. Even from where he stood, Jonathan noticed the way her scent changed. She half-turned to leave, then stopped. "Oh, I almost forgot!" She pulled a small vial of red liquid from her pocket and set it on the desk. "This is for Matt."

"What is it?"

"I uh, swiped a healing potion from the hospital," she explained, "and modified it a little. It will grow his hand back."

"Thank you," he told her, "I'm sure Matt will appreciate the gesture."

"Probably not right away," Angel said, "apparently regrowing a limb hurts like hell."

"He'll manage," Jonathan assured her. "Where are you going to go?"

"No idea."

"Here," Jonathan said, scribbling his number down on a loose piece of paper, "this is my home number, and my personal cell number. If you need anything, anything at all, just call and I will do my best."

He handed her the piece of paper. Angel took it and stuffed it in her pocket.

"I will," she said. "And thanks, for everything. It was nice to be able to talk to someone about this stuff."

"Anytime," he told her.

CHAPTER 47

Caleb didn't get back to his new hotel room until late that evening. They'd searched for Angel near the hospital, and anywhere else in the city they could think of, but they hadn't found her, which really didn't surprise him. What did surprise him was how calm he felt about the whole situation. He wasn't actually worried she was gone; he was more worried about why she'd left in the first place. This past week, he'd learned while she was incredibly strong when it came to magic and fighting, she was emotionally fragile. Considering she'd been perfectly fine before her mother showed up, Caleb had to assume Elizabeth was to blame. He'd tried calling her using the number he got from Scott, but as soon as he'd identified himself, she'd hung up and blocked his subsequent calls. So now he was lying in bed, with no idea where Angel was, no idea what was wrong, and no idea how to fix it all. He was contemplating a hot shower to help himself get to sleep when his phone started to ring. He dashed out of bed and started rifling through his discarded clothes, pulling the device from his pocket. No name or number showed up on Caller ID, but he answered it anyway.

"Hello?"

"Hi," came Angel's voice from the other end of the line.

"Angel, are you okay?"

"Yes. No. I don't know." She paused, sighing heavily. "I'm sorry I left without saying anything."

"It's alright, I understand," he told her. "Where are you? I'll come pick you up."

"I...I don't think that's a good idea."

"Oh?"

"It's not you! I swear. There's just some things I need to figure out, and I need some time alone to do that."

"Alright. Take as much time as you need."

"You're not mad?"

"Do you love me?"

"Yes," she replied without hesitation.

"And I love you. And I'm not mad. I can't pretend to know what you're going through right now, but if you say you need time to figure things out, then you should take as much as you need. And I know you'll talk to me about it when you're ready."

"Thank you."

"You're welcome. Let me know if you need anything."

"I will. I should probably go now."

"Wait," he said, "there's something I need to tell you."

"What is it?"

Caleb took a deep breath and said the words he'd been agonizing over for months, realizing now nothing had ever felt so right.

"You're my Mate."

CHAPTER 48

She was furious. She stormed around the small house she'd been using as a nest, throwing whatever she could get her hands on. Picture frames and dinner plates hit the wall and smashed into little pieces that littered the floor. The few vampires she allowed inside scattered quickly, not wanting to become the next thing she got her hands on. She cursed, loudly and colorfully, in each of the half-dozen languages she'd learned over her long life. The Master Alpha lived. Not only that, casualties at the conference had been minimal. Decades of planning, years of preparation, and the attack had failed miserably.

She let out one last wordless scream and fell silent. She stopped, taking a few deep breaths, even though she didn't actually need to breathe. For some reason, the action was still soothing. She crossed the room and snatched her cell phone off the kitchen counter, dialing a number she knew by heart. It rang twice, then he picked up.

"Hello."

"Have you seen the news?"

"Yes."

He didn't say anything else for a solid minute, and she started to feel her rage building again.

"And!?" she prompted.

"What do you want me to say? The Master Alpha is still alive."

"It wasn't my fault. They had a witch working for them. A very powerful witch. How the hell was I supposed to plan for that? I had dozens of vampires, over a hundred zombies. That should have been more than enough."

"But it wasn't."

"Why the hell are you so calm? We failed. We didn't kill the Master Alpha, and now he knows someone is after him. We'll never get another chance at him like this again."

"Of course we will. The Master Alpha is not one to stay safe while others are in danger. If his packs are threatened, he will fight to keep them safe."

"And what if he keeps that witch around, huh?"

"I'll deal with her."

"But–"

"I said, I will deal with the witch. You take whoever you have left and move north. I'll contact you with further instructions."

Made in the USA
Middletown, DE
07 August 2021

45551388R10130